Sherlock's Home

As Neil wound down his window and craned his head outside to get a closer look, he could hear the dog's excited barks as he ran. At first, Neil couldn't see the person the police dog was supposed to be chasing. Then the wavering torchlight caught a shadowy figure running along the hedge by the road.

"Let's get out and help!" Neil said eagerly.

His father quickly put a restraining hand on his arm. "No, Neil. For all we know, that man could be armed," he hissed. "We could lend a little light to things, though . . ."

Bob flicked their headlights on to full beam. He rolled the Range Rover down off the verge and began inching very slowly forwards towards the scene of the action . . .

Titles in the Puppy Patrol *series*

More Puppy Patrol stories follow soon

Puppy Patrol
Sherlock's Home

Jenny Dale

Illustrated by

Mick Reid

A Working Partners Book

MACMILLAN CHILDREN'S BOOKS

Special thanks to Lorna Read

First published 1999 by Macmillan Children's Books
a division of Macmillan Publishers Limited
25 Eccleston Place, London SW1W 9NF
Basingstoke and Oxford
www.macmillan.co.uk

Associated companies throughout the world

Created by Working Partners Limited
London W12 7QY

ISBN 0 330 37634 9

1 3 5 7 9 8 6 4 2

A CIP catalogue record for this book is available from
the British Library.

Typeset in Bookman Old Style by SX Composing DTP, Rayleigh, Essex
Printed and bound in Great Britain by Mackays of Chatham plc, Kent

Chapter One

"**C**areful, Dad!" Neil Parker clutched the pet carrier on his knee firmly, steadying it as the King Street Kennels Range Rover hit a flooded pothole in the road.

"I'm going to speak to Councillor Jepson about the state of this road," Bob Parker complained angrily. Neil's father jerked the steering wheel to steady the vehicle and keep it firmly under control as they crawled through the blackness. "Imagine if I'd been driving any faster? That carrier might have hit the wind-screen!"

"I hope Pepé's all right," said Neil worriedly. It was too dark a night to see the tiny occupant inside the carrier, but the little short-haired chihuahua was very quiet. Neil didn't know if this was a good sign or not.

Dogs were the most important things in Neil's life. His parents ran King Street Kennels and rescue centre near the small country town of Compton. He'd become very interested in dogs' health problems and illnesses since his own dog, Sam, a superb black and white Border collie, had developed a heart condition.

Pepé, one of their many current boarding dogs, had looked seriously ill less than half an hour ago when Neil had found him in his pen twitching and shaking. Now Neil was impatient to get him to the vet as fast as possible. That was, if the driving sleet and battering wind would allow them to get to Mike Turner's surgery at all. There was so much icy mush blowing onto the windscreen that the wipers were scarcely able to do their job.

The gale gathered strength as it blew across the open country fields. A blast of wind howled outside and Neil felt the vehicle lurch. Bob held the wheel steady.

Suddenly, like a lightning flash, a powerful beam of light lit up the inside of the car.

Dazzled, Neil turned his head away from the bright light.

"What the . . . ?" Bob stamped his foot on the brakes.

The tyres of the Range Rover screeched on the slippery road surface and the heavy vehicle skidded to the right.

Neil flung both arms round the pet carrier on his lap and held on tight as the Range Rover hit the verge, lurched upwards and then came to a stop with a jolt, leaving two wheels planted firmly halfway up the grassy bank.

"What on earth was that?" Bob exclaimed in a shocked tone. "I wasn't sure if it was another vehicle coming straight for us or not. Sorry, Neil. Are you and Pepé OK?"

"Yes, don't worry." Neil looked down at the carrier. "I didn't drop him." Gathering his wits, Neil strained to see out of the murky windscreen. The wipers were still struggling to clear the view as the car engine hummed eerily in the darkness. "Look, it's the police! I wonder what's going on?"

The flash of light had come from the powerful torch carried by a police officer. Further along the road, Neil saw him running out of the driveway of a large, isolated house. The torch

3

beam picked out the blurred shape of a speeding dog that was hurtling ahead of the officer down the country road.

"It looks like Jasper!" Neil exclaimed.

"Then that must be Sergeant Moorhead," Bob replied. Jasper was Compton's talented and popular police dog. The long-serving six-year-old German shepherd and the local sergeant with whom he lived were inseparable.

As Neil wound down his window and craned his head outside to get a clearer look, he could hear the dog's excited barks as he ran.

"Chase, Jasper!" Sergeant Moorhead shouted

4

urgently, before speaking rapidly into his radio.

At first, Neil couldn't see the person the police dog was supposed to be chasing. Then the wavering torchlight caught a shadowy figure running along the hedge by the road. In the distance, a second beam of light appeared and another officer could be seen racing towards the scene from the opposite direction.

"Let's get out and help!" Neil said eagerly.

His father quickly put a restraining hand on his arm. "No, Neil. For all we know, that man could be armed," he hissed. "Best leave chasing and catching criminals to the police. We could lend a little light to things, though . . ."

Bob flicked their headlights on to full beam. He rolled the Range Rover down off the verge and began inching very slowly forwards towards the scene of the action.

Now the escaping man could be seen more clearly. He was heading for a car parked against a field gate. Both Sergeant Moorhead and his colleague were having difficulty keeping their feet on the icy road and before either officer could apprehend him, the man had reached his car and yanked open the driver's door.

But he hadn't reckoned with the speed of four legs!

Jasper was faster and soon upon him. With an enormous bound, the dog's jaws gripped the sleeve of the man's jacket. The big German shepherd growled menacingly and pulled hard, preventing the man from climbing into the car.

Neil watched open-mouthed as the struggle between man and beast continued.

The powerful, muscular dog used all his strength to tug, his pads scrabbling for purchase on the slushy road, while the man swore and struck out desperately with both feet and his free hand.

Just as it seemed that Jasper was winning and would manage to hold on until one of the officers reached him, the sleeve tore off the man's jacket. Finding himself free at last, he hurled himself into his car.

Jasper jumped up after him.

Then came a sound that made Neil feel momentarily sick – the simultaneous slam of a car door and agonized shriek of the dog whose paw had been trapped and crushed in it.

As Neil watched, transfixed with horror, the car door opened and Jasper, yelping in pain, fell onto the road. Then everything seemed to happen at nightmare speed. The door slammed again and the car engine roared into life, shooting forward towards the Range Rover.

Jasper disappeared underneath the wheels.

"Nooooo!" screamed Neil.

The driver must have felt the bump as he ran over the injured dog, but he didn't stop.

Before Neil could leap out to Jasper's aid, a motorbike roared past from behind, and a gust of wind rustled Neil's hair. It swerved violently to get out of the path of the car as it hurtled towards them, only just missing the dark shape that was lying so still on the gleaming wet road. It was a miracle that the motorbike wasn't hit too. The rider stopped for a moment, appeared to quickly take in what was going on around him, then flung his machine round and sped off again in pursuit of the disappearing car. The bike whizzed past Neil's ear for a second time.

Neil instinctively thrust the pet carrier onto his dad's lap and leapt from the Range Rover, ignoring Bob's cries to come back at once. Freezing sleet lashed his face and crept down the neck of his jacket as he neared the injured dog.

Sergeant Moorhead was already bending by the dog's side, shining the torch over him. The second officer was nowhere to be seen.

"Is he . . ." gasped Neil, "is he OK?"

"The car went right over him," the sergeant said with a catch in his voice. The policeman seemed reluctant to touch him as if he was scared that he would hurt the dog further.

Neil felt a lump form in his throat. *How could anybody be so cruel?* In the light from the torch and the Range Rover headlamps, Neil could see dark blood oozing from Jasper's nose and mouth. He knew it didn't look good. The police dog's crushed paw was also bleeding badly.

The noise of another car engine made Neil look up for a second, and he saw a police car drive after the fleeing assailant and motorbike.

Then Bob crouched down and joined them. Neil and the sergeant shuffled along to make room for him. Bob quickly felt for a pulse amongst the fur on the dog's neck. "He's still alive. Let's get him straight to the surgery."

"I'll come with you," said the sergeant, relief in his voice.

"We'll need to move him as little as possible," said Bob urgently. "He may have back injuries. Neil?"

"Yes, Dad?"

"Call Mike and tell him we've now got *two* patients for him." He took his mobile phone out of his pocket and handed it over. "Tell him what's happened so that he's prepared. This is an emergency."

"Thanks, Bob," said the sergeant. He tentatively reached out his hand and began stroking the dog's head gently.

Neil stood up and looked around. He could still barely believe what was happening. He stabbed a finger in the direction that the car and motorbike had driven off. "But . . . won't that man be getting away?"

The police sergeant remained calm. "Constable Grey will follow him. My place is here. I need to . . . look after Jasper."

Neil punched out Mike's number on the phone and made the call for help.

Oblivious to the sleeting rain, Bob took off his jacket and laid it on the road, waterproof side down. Then, very gently, working together, he and Sergeant Moorhead carefully slid the heavy body of the unconscious German shepherd onto the jacket. Holding it taut between them, they carried it towards the Range Rover. Neil finished the call and pocketed the phone, then rushed to open the rear door to the dog cage.

"I'll get in with him to stop him being thrown about," the sergeant insisted.

High-pitched yaps were coming from the abandoned Pepé.

Neil felt a pang of guilt. In the heat of the moment, Neil had almost forgotten about him. Bob spoke soothingly to the tiny dog through the mesh of the carrier. The dog looked nervous and his shiny, short, pointed muzzle glistened in the shadows of the carrier. Bob handed it to Neil to hold as he got into the driver's seat and pulled the door closed. Neil strapped himself in and, at last, they were on their way again towards Compton.

Neil suspected that the sergeant probably didn't want to talk about the assault on Jasper, but he was desperate to make sense of the drama that had just happened. He couldn't resist asking the questions that were burning in his mind. "Sergeant Moorhead, I'm sorry about Jasper. But who was that man? Why were you at the house?"

"Neil!" said Bob, angrily.

"No, it's OK, Bob." The sergeant continued stroking Jasper as he spoke. "We had an anonymous tip-off that the house was going to be burgled tonight. It's the weekend home for a city businessman, who we know owns rather a lot of very valuable antique jewellery."

The sergeant's account was interrupted when Jasper made a sickening, throaty, choking noise.

Neil stiffened. "Hang on in there, boy," he sighed. "We'll be there soon."

"Yes, we're nearly there," said Bob.

The policeman nodded then continued. "Anyway, we thought we'd stake the place out and catch him red-handed. Trouble was, he'd arrived before us and was already in there taking what he was after. When we saw torch-light moving about inside we moved in. He must have heard us and tried to make a run for it." The sergeant inhaled deeply. "That's when you arrived, I think. And you saw what happened to Jasper . . ." His voice trailed off.

"We're here!" announced Neil quickly, cutting across the sergeant's grief.

As they drew up on the gravel drive outside the veterinary surgery, Neil saw Mike Turner standing in the doorway, watching out for them. He rushed towards them. *We've made it*, Neil thought. Now Jasper and Pepé could get the medical attention they both desperately needed.

Bob yanked open the rear car door and Mike climbed in beside the sergeant. Neil leaned back to watch. The vet bent over Jasper, felt for a pulse, tentatively listened for a heartbeat, then turned to the three concerned faces that stared so hopefully at him.

"I'm sorry," he said, shaking his head, "it's too late."

"No, Mike!" cried Neil. "He was breathing a minute ago. Check him again."

Sergeant Moorhead lowered his head.

Bob rested his hand on the policeman's shoulder.

"Neil," the vet persisted, "there's nothing I can do. I'm afraid he's gone. Jasper is dead."

Chapter Two

For the rest of that tragic evening, Neil felt like a zombie. He was numb with grief for poor Jasper and Sergeant Moorhead. He knew he would *never* forget the stricken look on the sergeant's face when Mike Turner told him that the police dog was dead.

"You go on inside with Pepé, Neil," said Bob Parker. "We'll take care of this."

Neil sat alone in the surgery with the carrier on his knee. Inside it, Pepé seemed to have become very lively. He was scrabbling at the wire front, yapping. If he could have scratched or wriggled his way out, he certainly would have done.

When Neil poked his fingers through the wire

13

and ran them along his smooth, glossy coat, Pepé shifted round and his warm tongue licked them, making Neil feel a little better.

Eventually, Mike and Bob reappeared.

"The sergeant's been picked up and taken back to the station," said Bob. "Jasper's going to stay here tonight." He ran a hand over his dripping hair and beard. "I feel as if I've been in a shower with all my clothes on," he said. "And look at you!"

Neil suddenly realized how wet he was. He was cold to the bone and his socks and shoes were soaked through.

"You'd better get home quickly or you'll catch pneumonia," Mike said. "Let me just take a look at this little chap here. What did you say his symptoms were when you found him?"

Despite his grief for Jasper, Neil tried to focus on Pepé's plight. "He looked as if he was having a fit," he explained. "He was trembling all over and his mouth was frothing. And he was coughing and wheezing, too. I was really worried about him. I can't understand how he could have recovered so quickly. He seems so much better now."

Neil remained anxious as Mike gently lifted the tiny dog out of the carrier and placed

him on a large examining table.

"There doesn't seem to be *anything* the matter with him," the vet said. "His temperature's fine and his heart and breathing are normal." Mike gently touched several different places over the dog's small body. "And he doesn't seem to be in pain anywhere." Looking into Pepé's mouth, he added, "He is salivating slightly, though. See this dribble on his mouth? I think it's best if he stays in overnight for observation. I'll give you a ring in the morning with an update."

"So there's no need to worry just yet?" asked Bob.

"No, I don't think so. Chihuahuas can be . . ."

"Yes?" said Neil, hurriedly.

"Well, they're great tremblers, you know. They just have to get a bit scared or overexcited, and they start to quiver. So don't worry about that," Mike said.

"Come on." Bob put an arm round Neil's shoulders. "Let's get home. Mike's quite right, we'll catch something terrible if we don't get out of these wet clothes soon."

"And what have you two been up to?" scolded Carole Parker, as her husband and son dripped their way into the front hall of their house back at King Street. "You look terrible!"

Sam the Border collie roused himself from a slumber by the living room fire and padded up to Neil, wagging his tail. Jake, Sam's young son, dived out from behind the sofa and curled himself around Neil's wet legs. Jake was always full of energy – no matter what the hour or situation.

Neil raised a smile and gave the puppy a pat on the flank, then ordered him to sit. He crouched down and hugged Sam, grateful for his faithful affection. Over his head he was aware of Bob and Carole talking about

Jasper's fatal accident.

Carole was devastated by the news. "Hot showers right now for the pair of you," she ordered in a choked voice. "I'll make some cocoa to warm you up."

Bob and Neil were soon back downstairs again, feeling better in body but not in spirit.

Emily, Neil's nine-year-old younger sister, had been upstairs getting ready for bed, but she dashed down again in her slippers and dressing gown when she heard the commotion, and joined everybody in the living room.

"How's Pepé?" she asked brightly. "What was it?" Then, noticing the gloomy faces, her expression changed. "Oh, no! It's not serious, is it?" she asked in horror.

Neil struggled to speak. His thoughts flashed back to Jasper's terrible, agonized cries of pain when the car had mangled him earlier that evening.

"Em, I've got some bad news," said Bob sadly. "It's not about Pepé – he's fine, we think."

"It's Jasper . . ." mumbled Neil.

Breakfast the next morning was a solemn affair in the Parker house, especially as there was one further person who still had to be told – Neil and Emily's five-year-old sister, Sarah. She immediately burst into tears and refused to be comforted, even when Jake licked her ankle under the table – something which normally made her shriek and giggle.

Emily put her arm round her. "Come on, Sarah. We're all very sad, but crying can't bring him back. Let's go and see what Fudge is up to, shall we?"

But Sarah showed no interest in her pet hamster and even refused her breakfast. Jasper was all she could think of.

Neil was off his food too. He hadn't slept well and it wasn't just because of his horrible experience the previous night. For the last few evenings they had all been disturbed by heart-rending howls from the rescue centre. The culprit was Mickey, a black and white mongrel. Everyone was doing their best to make him feel loved and help him settle in, but so far with no result. That night, the howls had affected him worse than usual. They made him think about Jasper and the terrible sound he had made when he got trapped in the car door.

"So Compton is without a police dog," Bob said as he munched on a piece of toast.

How could Dad eat at a time like this?

thought Neil. He pushed his cereal bowl across the table.

"How about Sergeant Moorhead having a rescue dog?" suggested Emily. "Couldn't the police use one of those?"

Bob shook his head. "I'm afraid not. Police dogs have to be specially trained from when they're puppies. And they don't use just any old breed, either. It's mostly German shepherds."

"No police dog could ever be as good as Jasper was," Neil said wistfully.

Sarah gave a loud sniff. "Will Jasper be buried here, Dad?"

"I think Sergeant Moorhead will have to decide that, pet," said Bob. "He might like to bury Jasper in his own garden."

At that moment, Neil felt a tug under the table as Jake chewed on one of his shoelaces. "Jake, get off!" Despite his low spirits, he reached down and playfully fondled Jake's ears. "Time for your walk, I think," he said, grateful for an opportunity for a breath of fresh air.

"Be quick, Neil, or you'll be late for school," said Carole. "And let's all try and cheer up a bit, shall we? It's stopped raining and look, the sun's even coming out."

Neil tried to smile, but he knew it was going to take a little while longer before he started laughing and joking again.

After school that afternoon, Neil and Emily lounged around in front of the television. Neil's hand trailed over the side of his armchair and he absent-mindedly stroked Jake's smooth head.

"Did you notice anything funny about Kate this morning?" he asked suddenly.

Emily looked up from her dog magazine. Neither of them ever missed visiting the kennel blocks and rescue centre before going to school. Kate McGuire, the longest-serving of their two full-time kennel maids, usually started work at the crack of dawn. Bev had only recently joined them, when the Kennels had expanded and a new, larger rescue centre had been built. Both of them were invaluable and the Parkers knew that King Street couldn't operate smoothly without them.

"Yes, I did!" said Emily indignantly. "She walked right past me and didn't say hello!"

"Same here," said Neil. "She just didn't seem to hear me. It was as if she was miles away."

Emily shrugged. "Perhaps she was just very busy."

"Maybe, but it's not like her to be rude," Neil pointed out. "She's normally so friendly."

Then Carole Parker popped her head round the door. "Are you talking about Kate?"

Neil and Emily nodded, and Carole came into the room and perched on the edge of the sofa. "Mmm. Kate asked if she could have a word with me today, actually." Carole paused and bit her lip. "She . . . well, she might be leaving us, I'm afraid."

"No!" Emily cried. "She can't possibly leave us or the dogs." Her face was white with shock.

"What's happened?" asked Neil. His mind was spinning. Whatever would they do without Kate? She'd been with them so long that she was almost part of the family. Her leaving was unthinkable.

"Well," explained Carole, "Terri McCall has been promoted at the local RSPCA office and her old officer's job will be vacant. Kate's been asked to apply for it."

Carole sighed heavily. She looked strained and anxious. Neil gave her a hug. "Don't worry. We'll help, Mum! I could leave school and then I could be with the dogs all day and—"

"Oh no, you won't!" Carole replied quickly. "It's not come to that yet!"

"Maybe she won't get the job," said Emily.

"But she *might*," said Carole miserably. "She's perfect for it, really. We all know that. We just have to accept that Kate won't be around for ever and we have no right to expect her to stay just because it makes our lives easier."

"It'll be impossible to replace her," said Neil.

"I know. I've tried changing her mind – but I've not had much luck so far. Anyway, I thought you should know the situation."

"Thanks, Mum," said Neil quietly.

"I must go. I need to have a word with Kate before she leaves tonight."

Carole went off, leaving Neil staring at his sister, their minds racing.

"I don't know how Kate could even *think* of leaving the dogs!" Neil erupted.

"She can still work with dogs at the RSPCA, though. And all kinds of *other* animals, too," Emily said. "Maybe that's what she wants."

"Maybe," said Neil. "But do you think *we* can have a go? To persuade Kate to stay?"

Emily's face developed one of her familiar fierce expressions that meant she was concentrating really hard. "Of course we can!" she said.

"Then let's go and find her!"

Neil and Emily rushed out into the courtyard but before they could reach the office where they thought she might be, Bev appeared with Mickey, the mongrel who'd kept them awake all night.

"Hello, there!" she said cheerfully, and even though they were still shocked and unhappy about Kate, Neil and Emily couldn't help smiling back at her.

Bev was one of those people whom you took to straight away. She was older than Carole, but was so small, wiry and speedy that at times Neil forgot that and thought she was nearer his

own age! In the short time she had been at the kennels, she had thrown everything into her new job. She got on well with Kate, and the dogs loved her – but there was no way she would be able to manage all the work on her own if Kate left.

"It's a funny old business with Pepé, isn't it?" said Bev.

Neil nodded. "Even Mike hasn't a clue what was wrong."

"Well, your dad brought him back from the surgery this afternoon," said Bev, smiling. "So he's settled in his pen again if you want to go over there and see him. I've just taken Mickey for a long walk in the hope that he'll be too tired to bark tonight."

"Let's hope so!" said Emily.

Bev and Mickey went off in the direction of the kennels and Neil and Emily continued towards the kennels office. As they approached the door, two raised voices drifted out from inside. Both sounded agitated.

"Don't be ridiculous, Kate," they heard their mother say. "You're just as good as Bev. In some ways you're better, because—"

"But I don't *feel* it, Carole!" Kate cut in.

Neil knew that they shouldn't eavesdrop, but

neither of them could help it!

"Bev sometimes . . . makes me feel inadequate," continued Kate. "She's a *natural*. She's so good at what she does."

"She's a lot older than you," said Carole.

"I just feel it's time I left. Please don't think I'm not grateful, Carole. You and Bob are *experts* at what you do and you've been marvellous to me, you really have. But I'm fed up with feeling I'm not as good as everybody else. That's why I'd like to try for the RSPCA job. I feel I'd have something special to offer."

Neil and Emily listened as the conversation carried on, with their mother vainly trying to convince Kate that she was amazingly good at her job, and Kate refusing to believe it.

When they heard their father calling them they reluctantly dragged themselves away and ran back towards the house.

Bob was in the kitchen boiling the kettle. "I've just been on the phone to Sergeant Moorhead," he said.

"What is it?" asked Emily excitedly. "Have they found that horrible man who killed Jasper?"

"Not quite," said Bob. "But they've traced his car. It was stolen from a car park in

Colshaw yesterday afternoon."

"No sign of the dog murderer, then?" grumbled Neil.

"'Fraid not. But I do have some other rather interesting news for you."

"Yes?" asked Neil. He felt as if nothing could interest him after all the drama he'd experienced over the last twenty-four hours.

"It's about the motorcyclist we saw last night. The one who provided the police with the burglar's car registration number."

"What about him?" Neil suddenly felt anxious about what his father might say next. "Who was it?"

"Somebody you know quite well . . ."

"Stop teasing, Dad," laughed Emily. "Tell us who it was."

Bob scratched his beard. "It was Mr Harding."

Neil's jaw dropped.

Emily sat down at the table with a thud. "Not *the* Mr Harding? The ex-policeman Neil caught stealing antiques?"

Bob nodded.

"Jessie's owner," Neil croaked. "He's back."

"He sure is," said Bob.

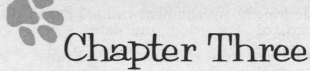

Chapter Three

N eil gazed at his father. "No! I don't believe it," he gasped in amazement. "I thought he was still in prison!"

"He was let out early for good behaviour," said Bob.

The previous year, Neil and his friend Chris from Meadowbank School had helped put Harding behind bars for his involvement with a gang of antiques robbers. Neil had gone in search of Harding after he had left his pregnant Airedale-cross bitch, Jessie, at King Street Kennels and failed to return for her. He'd found him tied up in a remote cottage, having double-crossed the gang. Since then, Neil had often wondered what had happened to Jessie and her pups. She was one of the best-trained dogs Neil had ever met.

"What a blast from the past!" said Emily.

Neil slowly began to get over the initial shock of discovering that Harding was a free man. "I suppose I always felt that Mr Harding wasn't really cut out to be a criminal," Neil said. Harding had been a police dog trainer before turning to crime. "He was too fond of dogs to be a *really* bad man."

Bob Parker gave a short laugh. "Maybe you've discovered something that psychologists and historians would be fascinated to learn," he told Neil. "If you go to university, you should write something on the world's most evil people, and whether they had dogs or not!"

Emily cleared her throat. "Did Sergeant Moorhead say anything about Jasper?"

Bob's expression turned serious again. "Yes, he says he had a little ceremony for Jasper earlier this evening. He buried him in his garden. He wanted us to know. He was really grateful for our help and support yesterday."

Neil looked down. He didn't want his dad to see how upset he was. He swallowed hard and said, "I wish we'd been there."

"Some things have to be private, Neil. I'm

sure you understand," Bob said.

Neil did.

"He says he's going to have to get a new dog very soon, but it's going to be hard for him to get used to working with a different one."

"Yes, there was something special between Sergeant Moorhead and Jasper – a bit like me and Sam," said Neil. "He really did love that German shepherd . . ."

"Will he have the choice of several dogs?" Emily asked.

"There won't be that many to choose from. Lots of dogs that start training prove unsuitable. Only the best make the grade. But I'm sure he could refuse one if he thought it wasn't suitable."

"How old are they when they start training?" Neil asked his father.

"A few months, I think. Sergeant Moorhead will know more about it than I do. Why don't you ask him next time you see him?" said Bob.

"I will. I'd like to know how they're trained. Perhaps I could pick up a few tips to pass on to Jake," said Neil.

"Looks like being another busy Saturday," said Carole the following morning as she glanced out

29

of the kitchen window. There was a long queue of noisy dogs and their owners waiting outside the old rescue centre.

"As usual!" said Emily, munching on her breakfast.

The old rescue centre had been converted into a walk-in dog clinic and was staffed by Mike Turner every Saturday morning.

"I hope he turns up soon," added Neil. "The noise is deafening."

Their chatter was interrupted by the kitchen door being flung open with a crash, and Bev rushing in. "Come quick! Pepé's having another fit," she panted.

Neil crossed the yard in record time and got to Pepé's pen ahead of everybody else. He was horrified to see the tiny brown chihuahua breathing so fast that it seemed as if his lungs would burst. The dog's rasping coughs made his mouth drip with saliva as he crept round the floor of the pen in a trembling circle.

"What is it?" he asked his mother urgently as he hastily unfastened the pen and rushed inside.

"I don't know. I've never seen anything like it," she replied, shaking her head.

Neil picked Pepé up and cradled his shivering

form. "I'll look after him while you see if Mike's arrived yet," he said.

"I think I just saw his car," Emily said.

Carole ran off leaving Neil to comfort the small, heaving body in his arms. Emily looked on worriedly.

A few minutes later, Carole was back with Mike just behind her. He took one look at Pepé and announced, "It looks like an asthma attack. Let me see." He took his stethoscope out of his bag and held it to Pepé's chest. "That's funny . . ."

Handing the stethoscope to Carole, he took Pepé from Neil, looked into the dog's eyes and ears and felt his chest and abdomen. "Does it say anything about asthma in his kennel notes?" he enquired.

The owner of every King Street Kennels resident had to fill in a questionnaire detailing their dog's dietary requirements, dates of vaccinations with copies of certificates, and information about any medical conditions the dog might suffer from. After a quick glance at his chart, Carole declared that Pepé's owner had previously given him a clean bill of health.

"Can a dog suddenly start suffering from asthma?" asked Neil.

"Asthma in dogs is a bit like asthma in humans – it can be brought on by stress," Mike informed him. "The symptoms are dribbling, coupled with acute respiratory distress. Has Pepé ever stayed in a kennels before?"

"He's been *here* before," said Carole. "Twice, in fact. And there wasn't anything wrong with him then."

"It can't be that, then. Something else must have caused it. Let's start by giving him an antihistamine injection. That will relieve his breathing difficulties," Mike said.

Once Pepé had had his injection, the little dog's breathing grew a lot calmer.

"Right. Let's have a really good listen to that chest of yours," said Mike. "You really are a tiny wee thing, aren't you? Can you hold him still for me, Neil?"

Mike listened intently to Pepé's chest. "This is weird," he said. He beckoned Neil closer. "Listen to this. Can you hear any wheezing in his lungs?"

Neil listened. "No, I can't. They sound clear to me," he said, handing the stethoscope back to Mike.

"Can I have a listen, too?" asked Bev . . . "You're right," she said. "He isn't wheezing at all."

"Whatever this little chap has got, then, it's not asthma. No wheeze means no asthma," Mike said. "And an asthma attack doesn't clear up like lightning, which is what happened to Pepé the other night. By the time you brought him in, he seemed fully recovered. There's got to be some other explanation . . ."

"What has he got, then?" Bev asked eagerly.

Mike picked Pepé up and examined him all over. Suddenly, he cried, "Aha!"

"What have you found?" Neil asked him.

"Have a look yourself," Mike said, carefully lifting up one of Pepé's front legs.

Neil looked. Right in the spot where the leg joined the body was an itchy-looking pink patch.

"It's an allergic rash," said Mike. "I'll give you some cream to rub on. Pepé is allergic to *something* in his environment. The trouble with allergies is that the symptoms don't show until you're in contact with whatever you're allergic to. The whole area of allergy is a pretty mysterious one."

"What on earth can Pepé be allergic to?" Carole wondered despairingly.

"Dust, paint, his bedding . . . It could be one of many things. The only way of finding out for sure is to do tests, but I really need his owner's permission as they're quite expensive. For now, I think it's better for me to treat the symptoms until she comes back."

"What can we do?" asked Neil.

"Well, you could help by keeping a close eye on him and seeing if you can identify anything that might be sparking it off," Mike replied. "Examine his pen, his bedding; change his diet, too. It could be that they've changed the formula in the dog food. You never know."

As Mike was putting away his stethoscope in his bag, he paused for a moment before lifting out a dog collar and lead. He stared at them thoughtfully.

"Whose are those?" asked Emily.

"They're Jasper's," said Mike.

Neil lay Pepé back in his basket and slowly took both items from the vet.

"Sergeant Moorhead left them in the surgery," said Mike. "I was going to drop them off at the police station this morning, but I didn't have time."

Neil fought back a spasm of grief. "I'll take them in to him," he offered. Neil had wanted to talk to the sergeant about what sort of a dog he was looking for as Jasper's replacement. Maybe he, or the King Street Kennels website, could help the police find a new dog. "Dad and I were already going into town later. Don't worry, I'll make sure he gets them."

Mike nodded solemnly. "Thanks, Neil."

As Neil and Emily entered the small reception area of the modern red-brick police station in Compton, Neil immediately spotted a familiar head of ginger hair. It was Mr Harding.

With a sense of shock, Neil realized that it had been nearly a year since he had last seen the ex-policeman. He remembered the frightening time when he was all alone with a tied-up Harding in a remote cottage, waiting for the police to arrive. Harding's dog Jessie had chosen that moment to go into labour. It had been touch and go for Jessie for a while, until Mike had operated on her and delivered the three pups – one large dog that had got stuck in her birth canal, and two bitches.

"Look, there's Mr Harding," whispered Emily.

"I don't want him to see me," Neil hissed and looked away. "He might be angry with me for getting him put in prison!"

But it was too late.

Harding had seen them. He said something to the duty officer who was manning the reception desk, then came over, looking rather sheepish.

Bob Parker arrived behind Neil and locked eyes with Mr Harding.

"Er, hello, Mr Parker," said Harding. "Hello, Neil. I gather you and your dad were a great help to Sergeant Moorhead the other night . . ."

"I hear you were, too," Bob replied with a very frosty expression on his face.

Neil glanced up at his dad then at Mr Harding. Neil could tell he wasn't at all pleased to be confronted with the ex-policeman. Neil had been in a great deal of danger back then and his parents blamed Mr Harding.

"I'm just waiting for the sergeant to arrive," Harding said. "I've got some fresh information for him."

"Really?" said Bob.

"Yes, but I'd like a word with you first."

Neil froze. Was Mr Harding about to be angry with him for handing him over to the police like he did? He decided to get in first. "Look, if it's about what happened, I had to do it—"

Harding shook his head. "Neil, don't worry. There's no hard feelings. I know you had to. I did wrong and was punished. Let's forget what's passed, eh?" Neil thought Mr Harding looked sincere – but he'd been misled by that expression before. "No, it's something different I wanted to talk to you about," Harding continued. "It's about Jessie. I've never really thanked you for what you did for her . . ."

Mr Harding looked ill at ease and Neil felt almost sorry for him. Despite everything that had happened, Neil couldn't help liking Mr Harding – even though he was a criminal. Anybody who had witnessed his love and concern for Jessie, and the Airedale cross's obvious devotion to him, would have known

Harding for a true dog lover. And Neil had all the time in the world for dog lovers.

"What happened to her pups, Mr Harding?" Neil asked.

"They were real beauties." Mr Harding's eyes shone with pride. "They all found good homes. But it's thanks to you that they were born at all."

"I'd love to see Jessie again," said Neil. The words were out of his mouth before he could stop himself.

Emily gulped and Bob suddenly glared at him.

Neil couldn't help it, though. He'd grown so attached to Jessie during her stay at King Street Kennels and he *did* ache to see her again. After Harding's arrest, his sister had taken her in but Neil was glad that she and her beloved master were now reunited.

"I'm sure Jessie would like to meet you again, too," said Harding. "Why don't you and your father drop by some day soon? Even this afternoon, if you can make it. I know Barbara would be pleased to meet you."

"Who's Barbara?" enquired Neil. "Have you got another dog?"

Harding laughed. "No, she's my wife. We got

married just a month ago but we've known each other for years. We're living here in Compton now. In Forthlyn Grove on the edge of town. D'you know it?"

Neil nodded. "I'd love to come," he said, trying to avoid his father's eyes. He knew his dad wouldn't be at all keen to go.

Just then, Sergeant Moorhead came in. Bob was the first to greet him and ask how he was.

"Very sad," he replied. "I've had dogs before, but never one like Jasper. The dog that replaces him will have to be really special."

Neil stepped forward. "Sergeant, Mike asked me to bring these in for you. You left them at the surgery," Neil said. He handed over the collar and lead and saw the sorrow in the sergeant's eyes as he thanked him.

"I'll let you know if I hear of a suitable dog. How old does he have to be?" Bob asked the sergeant.

"Under a year. The sooner his training can start, the better." Then Sergeant Moorhead spotted Harding, who was waiting by the desk. "I'd better go and see what news he's brought me," he said. "And Neil . . . thanks for these." He lifted up Jasper's collar and lead. "I'll keep them as a souvenir of the best dog I've ever known."

Chapter Four

Over lunch that day, Neil tried hard to persuade his father to let him visit Jessie and Mr Harding. "But Dad, he's OK now – he's helping the police, he's on their side," he argued.

Bob seemed reluctant to trust him. "I'm not so sure," he insisted. "Don't you think it could be more than just coincidence that he just happened to be passing on Thursday night while the robbery was going on? He could have been involved in the robbery. That would mean that he might be partly to blame for Jasper's death!"

"No way!" exclaimed Neil. "He loves dogs. Look how good he is to Jessie! He'd never do anything to hurt one. I don't think he had anything to do with it."

Bob gave a grunt of disagreement.

"All I want is to go and see Jessie, just once," he said.

"And me," Emily joined in.

"What do you think, Mum?" asked Neil.

"Well, I suppose he'd hardly be likely to arrive at the scene of a crime as the getaway man on a motorbike!" said Carole.

"Exactly," said Neil. "He's got a wife now, too. He's got a new life. I'm sure he's made a fresh start, Dad."

"He did put you in a great deal of danger, Neil," said Bob. "But, I suppose a wife might be a good influence on him . . ."

"Like I am on you, you mean?" Carole teased Bob.

"What do you think, Sam?" Neil turned to the Border collie, who was noisily scratching himself.

Sam looked at Neil and barked. Neil laughed. "Remember Jessie?" he said. Sam's ears pricked up. "Would you like to see Jessie again, Sam? One bark for no, two for yes."

It was a long time since Neil had used the signs he had taught Sam. He didn't know if he would remember them. He had taught him to "count" by moving his hand in a certain way; once for one bark, twice for two, and so on. Sam's fantastic memory brought the correct response right away: "Woof, woof!"

Carole laughed. "That's not fair," she said. "How can anyone resist Sam?" Then her face grew more serious. "I've never forgotten Jessie. She was probably the best-trained dog who ever stayed here. And I don't say that lightly. I wonder if she'll ever have any more pups? She went through such a bad time giving birth, poor girl."

Neil smiled to himself. He had a feeling he was winning the battle. "Mum," he persisted, "I promise you I'll find out every detail about Jessie and let you know as soon as I come back."

Carole exchanged a stern look with Bob, but then her face softened a little and she let out a little sigh. "I suppose if your father supervised a short visit, then there would be no harm in that."

Neil and Emily smiled at each other. Result!

That afternoon, Neil and Emily were escorted by their dad to Mr Harding's new house at Forthlyn Grove.

Neil rang the bell and called Jessie's name through the letter box, and was rewarded with an outburst of excited barking. A pretty woman with blond hair answered the door and introduced herself as Barbara Harding.

"I'm so pleased to meet you all. James has told me all about how you helped Jessie," she said. "He really is grateful to you for saving Jessie's life. Aren't you, darling?"

Mr Harding came down the hallway behind her and stood behind his wife. "Yes, I certainly am," he said. "Now, come on. Listen to that welcome you're getting!"

Neil could hear frantic barks and thuds as Jessie tried to open the door of the living room. As soon as Harding turned the handle, she pushed her way out and ran straight to Neil, who held out his hand for her to lick.

The golden-brown Airedale cross looked the picture of health, so unlike the last time he had seen her, shortly after her pups had been delivered by Caesarean section in Mike Turner's surgery. Then, she had looked thin and stressed. Now, she looked a new dog. *I bet it's because Mr Harding's back*, thought Neil, as he tangled his fingers in her curly coat. "Good girl, Jessie," he said. "Now, sit!"

Jessie obeyed immediately. Neil took a dog treat out of his pocket and held it in the air. Jessie remained in a sitting position, though her wet black nose sniffed the air excitedly.

Emily laughed. "Poor Jessie. Look at her tail quivering."

"I bet Jake wouldn't last that long," Bob joked. "He'd have his nose in your pocket by now."

"Good girl," Neil repeated, walking backwards down the passageway till he arrived at the open kitchen door. Jessie stayed absolutely still, though she glanced at Harding once or twice. "Come, Jessie, come," Neil called. In three bounds, Jessie was there, happily taking the treat from Neil's hand.

"Who got her pups, Mr Harding?" asked Neil.

"An old colleague from my dog training days, Constable Lloyd, had the little dog. He called him Freddie. He's settled in really well. As for the two bitches, you know Marcus Welham?"

Everyone did. He was a footballer who played for a major team and had a big house near Padsham. "Marcus has got Amber and his cousin bought Dawn. They've all settled in really well."

"You've done what you came here for, you two. You've seen Jessie and found out about the pups. I think it's time we were going," Bob said. He looked uneasy, standing in the Hardings' front hall.

"You can't go yet. There's someone else I want to introduce you to," Harding said eagerly. "Come this way . . ."

Neil and Emily went with Harding, and Bob had no choice but to follow them through.

Mr Harding led them all out of the kitchen into an extension which had been turned into a very professional-looking dog kennels with two pens. One was empty, but in the other was a young, very furry German shepherd, who cocked his head on one side and wagged his tail in a friendly greeting.

"Meet Sherlock. I *hope* he's going to be Compton's next police dog," announced Harding.

"Cool!" said Neil, crouching down in front of the pen. "What a great dog. How old is he?"

"Eleven months," Harding replied. "He belonged to a dog breeder I used to know when I worked for the London Met who's just had to retire because of illness."

"What age do police dogs start training?" Emily wanted to know.

"If they're taken on as puppies, they go and live with their handlers at about three months. They're assessed properly at around ten months, and when they're about a year old, they start their proper training.

"Sherlock's a natural. He's taken to everything, especially tracking. Police dogs have to be able to search all kinds of different places such as buildings, open countryside and woods, to recover missing kids, property – you name it. Sherlock's so eager to work, it's not true," Harding said fondly.

"Why don't you let him live in the house with

you?" asked Bob. Neil gave his dad a sharp look. Despite his reservations, his dad was obviously interested in finding out more about Sherlock, too.

"He mustn't get spoiled. He is, first and foremost, a working dog. He comes in for a while every day. The rest of the time is spent working him and playing with him. Both are equally important," Harding explained.

"Can I have a look at him?" asked Neil.

"Sure." Mr Harding opened the door of the pen. "Stay," he ordered. Sherlock's ears flicked. There was no mistaking the intelligence and understanding in his amber eyes. But he stayed, even though he must have been dying to run out into the garden.

"Here," Harding said.

Sherlock bounded out of the kennel and sat by Harding's feet. Jessie came up and sniffed him and the two dogs rubbed noses. Neil offered his fingers to be sniffed, then stroked Sherlock's head. He half expected him to jump up but he remained where he was, although he pricked his ears and looked up at Neil.

"He's very obedient," said Emily. "When's he going to go and live with Sergeant Moorhead?"

"Er, the sergeant doesn't know about him

47

yet. It didn't seem right, so soon after Jasper's death," Harding replied.

"You're not a police dog trainer any more. Will they still take a dog from you?" asked Bob.

"They know I *was* a good trainer. And the police do try out dogs offered to them by members of the public, or recognized dog dealers. They're always short of talented dogs, and if a dog shows he's intelligent enough and has the right personality, they may take him on for training. They're very choosy because it costs more than six thousand pounds to train a police dog and they don't want to waste their money," explained Mr Harding.

"Do they only take dogs, or do they train bitches as well?" Emily wanted to know.

"Either. Some forces prefer dogs, but bitches can make excellent police dogs too."

Emily got down and made a fuss of Sherlock, burying her face in his thick fur. He made her giggle when he licked her ear.

"It'll be a wrench when he goes," remarked Bob, giving Sherlock's head a stroke.

"Yes, it will. But I'd like to see him working properly," Harding said.

"I'd love to see what he can do," said Neil. "Why don't you bring him over to our place some time? We've still got Sam's old agility course."

"Maybe I'll do that," said Mr Harding. "I'm sure Sherlock would love to show off his skills." He rubbed the thick ruff round the German shepherd's neck and was rewarded with a wet wrist. "You should see him tracking. He's great," said Harding. "In fact, I don't think I've ever worked with such a brilliant dog. Would you like to see him jump?"

There was a large, solid-looking object towards the end of the tidy, well-presented garden. "You don't mean that, do you?" asked Emily. "It's enormous!"

"Two metres," Harding said. "Police dogs have to be able to clear a three-metre long jump and a one metre hurdle as well. Stay, Jessie!"

He gave Sherlock the order to climb the wall. Sherlock hurled himself at it and scaled it like a mountaineer, using his claws to help him. At the top, he turned his head and panted happily at his audience before leaping down the other side.

"Good boy!" Harding exclaimed, ruffling his fur and giving him a pat.

"Ace!" said Neil. "We're impressed!"

"That *was* excellent," said Bob. "You don't want to leave it too long before you tell Sergeant Moorhead about him. The force will be insisting he gets another dog very soon," he warned. "I'll put in a good word, if you like . . . tell him I've seen Sherlock and that he's worth a look."

"I'm sure the sergeant will fall in love with Sherlock as soon as he sees him," said Emily.

"Falling in love with him's not the most important thing," Bob pointed out. "It's how good he is at police work that really counts. Dog and handler do have to take to each other though, so it's a mixture of the two. Isn't that right, Mr Harding?"

"Yes, that's right. If a dog and a handler

didn't take to each other, the handler would be given another dog. The bond between them is ultra-important. The dog has to *want* to do anything his handler might ask of him, which may include dangerous situations involving weapons."

Neil couldn't bear to think of criminals using guns or knives on dogs.

"Thanks for letting us meet Sherlock and Jessie, Mr Harding, but we really have got to be getting back now," said Bob. He tugged on Neil's arm.

Neil and Emily tore themselves away reluctantly.

"Maybe I can come again to see Sherlock?" said Neil as he went back into the house.

"Maybe," replied Harding. "If it's OK with your parents."

"Maybe . . ." mumbled Bob as they said their goodbyes.

Chapter Five

Neil and Emily arrived back at King Street Kennels to discover their mum in an agitated state. She looked quite pale and anxious.

"We've got rats in the food store," she announced.

"Yuk!" said Emily.

"And you know how much I hate them. They terrify me," Carole said with a shudder.

"What happened?" asked Bob.

"It was Kate who discovered it. Tooth holes in the bottom of sacks of dog biscuits. And they'd made a real meal of the hamster food." The Parkers bought animal feed in bulk from their suppliers. "Come and see for yourselves," Carole said.

Sure enough, there was a neat hole in the bottom of the sack of Fudge's food and a little heap of nuts and seeds on the concrete floor.

"Damn!" Bob exploded. "Rats are all we need. If a customer were to see one, we could lose our good name."

"We can't put poison down, though, because of the dogs," Carole pointed out.

"How about getting a dog to do some ratting for us? Maybe we could borrow Tuff," suggested Neil. Tuff was a Jack Russell terrier belonging to a local farmer, Harry Grey. Jack Russells had a reputation for being good ratters and Tuff was one of the best.

"It's an idea," said Bob. "But I'm not at all sure Harry would be able to spare him. He's got too many rats and mice of his own and Tuff would have to live here for a while."

"Shame," said Neil. "I'm sure he would have enjoyed it."

"What are we going to do, then?" asked Carole.

"How about getting a cat?" Emily piped up.

"We couldn't possibly have a cat," snapped Carole. "It would drive the dogs crazy."

"Where's Kate?" Bob asked Carole. "We should ask her if she's actually seen one of these rats. We must be sure it is what we think it is."

"Oh, I gave her the rest of the day off," Carole replied. "She seems pretty depressed."

"*She's* depressed? What about *us*?" demanded Bob. "We're going to lose her and she'll be hard to replace. I still think we could help her change her mind."

Neil exchanged glances with Emily. They'd tried to corner her several times to help persuade her themselves, but had always been denied the chance. Someone else had distracted them, or the phone had rung, or she was just too busy to talk.

Just before dinner, Neil and Emily got ready to go out over the ridgeway behind the kennels to take Jake for a long walk. Emily suggested they take Pepé too, if he hadn't already been walked, so they went to the kennel block to find out.

They found Bev tidying up before she left for the day.

"Hi, Bev," said Neil. "Has Pepé been for his walk yet?"

Bev's blue eyes twinkled. "Not yet. I was sort of saving him for you," she said.

"That's great! I'll get his lead. D'you want us to take any of the others while we're about it?"

"I think Pepé will be quite enough. That little dog's like a jumping bean. He doesn't need vitamins – I think he's got springs in his paws," she grumbled.

Twilight was falling as Neil and Emily brought the dogs back to King Street. Pepé and Jake had both disgraced themselves in various ways, Jake by rolling in mud and Pepé by trying to wriggle down a rabbit hole.

"You're a chihuahua, not a dachshund," Neil had to remind him as he grabbed him by the wiggling hindquarters and dragged him out.

Neil put Pepé back in his pen in Kennel Block Two. He was just walking back across the courtyard to join Emily in the kitchen, when Jake suddenly gave a loud, excited bark and went dashing off in pursuit of something.

"Jake! Come here!" he called, but Jake took no notice.

The young collie skidded to a halt by the garden gate. Whatever it was had obviously got away under it – and had headed in the direction of their house!

Neil opened the gate and Jake ran inside. He stopped by Sam's favourite bush, then sniffed and whined. Neil couldn't see a thing in the fading light so he shrugged his shoulders and gave up, ushering Jake inside, into the warmth of the kitchen.

The following morning, Neil got up and found his father in a seething rage.

"Look at that!" he shouted, pointing out of the window into the back garden.

Neil looked. "What is it? I can't see anything."

"On the lawn!" thundered Bob.

Neil looked at the grass. There, leading from the very bush Jake had stopped at the previous night, was a neat row of molehills. He burst out laughing. He couldn't help it. His father looked at him furiously. "It's not funny," he complained.

"Yes it is," Neil retorted, and told his dad what had happened the previous night. "I took it for granted that Jake had seen a rat, but it was probably just a mole," he said.

"Moles eat insects. They don't eat grain or dog food," said Carole.

"I think we should set a trap in the feed store," suggested Neil.

"I don't know about that, but there's a certain young pup needs leading over to Red's Barn soon. My obedience class starts in half an hour. Don't be late," Bob reminded him.

Neil and Emily usually helped clean out the kennels on Sunday morning. They went in search of Kate and saw her heading for the rescue centre. "Quick, she's alone!" said Neil. It was the ideal opportunity to launch their campaign to stop Kate leaving.

They cornered Kate in one of the vacated pens, up to her elbows in soapsuds and water.

"Hi, Kate," Neil greeted her. "We've come to help."

"That's good. I could certainly do with it." Kate looked up and smiled, tossing her blond ponytail back over her shoulder.

Neil had planned to work up to the subject of her leaving gradually, but Emily pre-empted him.

"We can't believe you want to leave King Street!" she cried, sounding close to tears.

Kate went red. "Hang on, I don't know if I am leaving yet. I don't know if the RSPCA will have me," she said.

"Aren't you happy with us?" Emily continued in a choked voice.

"Of course I am," Kate replied. "But nobody can do the same thing for ever. We all need a change sometimes. Anyway, the RSPCA building is near where Glen lives." Glen was Kate's boyfriend.

"Oh, so Glen's the real reason," Neil said. "What a relief. We thought you were leaving because of Bev."

They waited for Kate's reply. She avoided their eyes and carried on playing with her hair. Then, finally, she said, "Bev *has* got something to do with it. I mean, I really like her and she's great with the dogs. Too good, that's the trouble. She's much better than me."

"Don't be stupid! You're both good at different things. That's why you're such a good team. We can't do without either of you. We really want you to stay, Kate. We'd miss you terribly if you left. So would the dogs."

Neil realized his words were falling on deaf ears as Kate lowered her eyes and busied herself with her cleaning. She was obviously dead set on getting the RSPCA job and there was nothing anyone could do about it.

There were five dogs in Bob's obedience class that Sunday morning. Jake was one of them and Neil was pleased when the young Border collie appeared to be responding to Bob's command to be quiet and stop barking.

The class was just ending when Carole walked up to the barn with Sergeant Moorhead. It was just a social call, the sergeant said. They were still searching for the thief who'd killed Jasper and they hadn't yet found the car.

"We're grateful to Mr Harding for getting the car number for us. Here it is. If you happen to spot it on your travels, let me know right away," said the sergeant, writing the car registration down for them. Bob and Neil promised they would.

This seemed like an ideal opportunity to tell the sergeant about Sherlock. Neil mouthed his name and his father gave him the nod.

"Has Mr Harding mentioned a dog called Sherlock to you?" asked Neil.

Sergeant Moorhead shook his head.

"He's a German shepherd and he's brilliant. Mr Harding's training him. I really think you should see him," Neil said eagerly.

"I'd have liked to, but it's too late, I'm afraid."

Neil's heart sank.

The sergeant went on. "I know it's only three days since Jasper was killed, but the force have already arranged to have a dog sent to me who's currently in the middle of his training. I'm obliged to give him first chance, I'm afraid. If he and I like each other, then that's it. His name's Oliver," the sergeant said. "He's arriving next weekend."

Neil brightened up again. If Oliver wasn't arriving for another week, then they had seven days to get Sherlock and the sergeant together. There had to be some way of doing it. Once he saw Sherlock, he was bound to be hooked and

Oliver would have to find another handler to work with.

"Come on, Em. Get your thinking cap on," Neil chivvied his sister. "There must be something we can come up with."

They were both in the kitchen sneaking hot chocolate and biscuits before their lunch.

"We could invite Mr Harding to come to the kennels with Sherlock," suggested Emily, "when we know Sergeant Moorhead's going to be here . . ."

Neil poured scorn on Emily's idea. "We *never* know when he's going to be here, dummy! He just pops in when he's off-duty. It's hopeless making any arrangements with him because he's likely to get called out on a job at any moment."

Emily huffed in annoyance. Then she said, "OK, I've got it. Mrs Harding can invite Sergeant Moorhead round for tea and chocolate cake, then Mr Harding could show him Sherlock."

Neil sighed. "Why should he want to go round there for tea? They're not exactly best buddies, are they? Anyway, he needs to be able to see Sherlock in action."

They sat in grumpy silence which was broken

only by Sam loudly lapping water out of his bowl. Jake whined to be let in so Emily opened the door and he scampered into the kitchen, wagging his tail excitedly.

Neil told him off when he jumped up and put his front paws on the table leg. "Down, Jake," he ordered. Neil laughed and scratched him between the ears, then ruffled the long, silky fur on his chest. "Will you never learn?" he said exasperatedly.

Neil and Emily decided to take Jake and Sam for a walk. Their mother was in the field, exercising some of the rescue dogs.

"Your father can't stop talking about Sherlock," she said. "I would love to see him."

"But you can, Mum," Neil told her. "All you have to do is ask Mr Harding. He'd love to show him off to you."

"I can't go round *there*," his mother replied.

"Why not?" Neil said. "You'd really enjoy talking to him. He knows an awful lot about dogs."

"The trouble is, I still have this thing about him," Carole confessed. "I can't help it. He put you in so much danger, Neil, and I'm not sure I want to become friendly with him. On the other hand, I'd like to see Jessie again. I'm hoping it won't be long before her pups become regular boarders of ours."

"Marcus Welham is away a lot. If his wife goes with him, we might get Amber to look after," Emily said hopefully.

"Why don't we invite Mr Harding to come here? He's never looked round properly before. He could see the kennels and bring Sherlock and Jessie with him, and you could watch Sherlock go round Sam's old agility course, if we can find all the pieces. Then you wouldn't have to make it a social occasion."

Carole looked thoughtful. "I suppose that would be OK. We'd be keeping things on a professional footing then, rather than making it personal."

"Can't he come this afternoon? I can't wait to see Sherlock again," Emily said.

"No. I've got far too much to do. Anyway, you only saw him yesterday," her mother replied. "Next weekend, perhaps . . ."

Both Neil and Emily would have been happy to see Sherlock and Jessie every day of the week, but they knew next weekend would have to do. It was very frustrating to have to wait so long.

Chapter Six

On Monday, Carole Parker was just starting the car to take Neil and his sisters to school when the phone rang.

Neil picked it up. It was Miss Thorn, the school secretary, and she sounded extremely harassed. She explained that there were some burst pipes in the main school building and the heating wouldn't work. School had to be cancelled for the day while the plumbers were called in.

Neil, Emily and Sarah couldn't believe their luck. Another day of freedom!

"Perhaps we could ask Mr Harding to come today," Neil suggested as they regrouped in the kitchen.

"Yes, please," echoed Emily and Sarah.

Their father was soon brought into the discussion. "I know your mother's dying to see if Sherlock's as good as we think he is . . . so, OK!"

Neil was delighted to discover that Mr Harding was free to come and visit. He seemed excited by the opportunity to show off Sherlock to Bob and Carole, who were such influential people in the local dog business. A couple of hours later, Neil rushed out of the house to greet him when he heard his car pull up outside the house.

Mr Harding walked with Jessie and Sherlock to the back of the house. Jessie seemed to recognize King Street Kennels immediately and soon ran around sniffing familiar smells and wagging her tail. She and Sam rubbed noses, but Jake surprised everyone by gluing himself to Jessie. He insisted on following her everywhere, giving little whines of pleasure when she licked him.

"He thinks he's one of her puppies," Mr Harding said.

Neil was relieved that Jake's adoration of Jessie really helped break the ice as far as his mother was concerned. She soon warmed to

Jessie and Neil could tell she found it difficult not to take an interest in the dog's well-being. "Are you going to let Jessie have another litter?" Carole enquired.

"No. She went through enough the last time. She's been spayed now," Mr Harding replied.

Sherlock looked magnificent. Neil crouched down and rubbed him under the chin while the German shepherd fixed him with his keen amber eyes. Carole adored him from the word go. She crouched down and examined him, looking at his eyes and the way he held his tail. She took a professional glance inside his mouth. "I can see that you clean his teeth," she said approvingly to Mr Harding. "You'd be surprised how many dog owners don't."

Bev and Kate came out to see who the visitors were and laughed at the antics of Jessie and Jake. Sam had gone back to the house and was lying in a rare patch of sunshine by the back door.

While Bev, Kate and Carole showed Mr Harding round the rescue centre, Neil asked his father to help him dig out all the old obstacles Sam used to practise his agility training on. It took quite a while to set up the plank and the jumps, then Neil went to fetch everyone.

Mr Harding led Sherlock into the field. The dog sat at his owner's feet, his eyes sparkling with excitement. His ears were pricked as he waited to be given the command to start.

As soon as his master spoke, Sherlock sped off like a rocket, with Mr Harding running along beside him giving him instructions and encouragement.

"Wow, look at him jump!" Emily shouted excitedly as Sherlock flew over the long jump.

The German shepherd was just approaching the hastily constructed wall, which Bob had helped to shore up, when all at once a shadow

appeared at his side – a sinuous, speeding, black and white one. As Sherlock made a leap for the top of the wall, another dog made it to the top before him and Neil gave a horrified cry. "Sam, no!"

With a hollow, sick feeling he watched the Border collie leap lightly down and run along the plank, showing the German shepherd the way. Then he ran over to Neil and sat at his feet, his pink tongue lolling and his ears pricked as if saying, "Aren't I clever?"

Emily was too horrified to speak.

"Neil!" thundered his father. "Didn't you make sure Sam couldn't get out of the kitchen?"

"But, Dad . . ." began Neil, faltering as he gently stroked the panting collie beside him.

"No buts. It was your responsibility to make sure Sam was shut safely indoors. You know how he loves obstacle courses. This was exactly what we didn't want him to do."

Before Sam's heart condition had been diagnosed, Neil used to enter the dog for every agility contest going. Sam adored them. But getting too excited was a serious risk to his health.

Neil had to forget about watching Sherlock complete the course as he walked Sam back to the house. His father's ominous parting words rang in his ears. "Calm Sam down before he collapses again." Neil couldn't help thinking that if anything happened to Sam now, it would all be his fault.

Neil sat with Sam for the remainder of the afternoon, but he didn't appear to have suffered any ill effects from his sudden burst of strenuous activity – the very thing Mike Turner had insisted Sam must avoid.

Bev found Neil in the living room, and checked that Sam was OK. "You really missed something after you went in," she said. "Your mother wanted to see Sherlock do some tracking, so they let him sniff one of Sarah's gloves. Then Mr Harding led Sherlock away so that he couldn't see Sarah trailing her glove across the field and hiding it. He followed the scent, nose to the ground, and went straight for it. It was brilliant."

Neil sighed. "I wish I'd been there," he said.

Bev gave Sam a long stroke from his head down to the tip of his tail. "Poor old thing," she said.

Then Sarah came rushing in and threw her arms around Bev, nearly knocking her flying. It was common knowledge that Sarah adored the new kennel maid.

"Come on, little 'un. Let's take Jake for a walk, shall we?" she suggested, sensing that Neil would rather be left alone with Sam. Bev was uncannily good at sussing out the moods of both humans and dogs. Emily thought she was a bit psychic.

"I missed saying goodbye to Sherlock. And Jessie," Neil said when his mother came back to the house.

"I'm sure you'll be seeing them again. It's this old chap you need to concentrate on for the time being," she said. She knelt down beside Sam and checked his heart rate against her wristwatch.

"He's been fine this afternoon," said Neil.

Carole nodded. "Good," she said.

"So were you impressed with Sherlock, then?" asked Neil.

Carole smiled. "Very. He'll be as good a dog as Jessie soon. Mr Harding's a very good trainer, I have to admit it."

"I know," said Neil.

"He has good instincts about dogs, too. You know the problem we're having with Mickey howling at night? Well, he asked me if we knew who Mickey's previous owner had been. When I said he used to belong to a factory night shift worker, Mr Harding guessed what the problem might be."

"And what's that?" Neil wasn't sure what she was getting at.

"Well, he reckoned that Mickey was used to being alone at night but probably had a radio or television left on as company for him."

"That's really clever!" exclaimed Neil.

"Quite," admitted Carole.

"So I suppose you want a loan of my portable radio," sighed Neil. "It'll cost you, though."

"OK, what's the cost?" Carole enquired, with a grin.

"A new set of batteries," Neil replied.

"It's a deal!"

Mr Harding's suggestion for silencing Mickey worked a treat, and the Parkers – and the dogs, too – had a peaceful night's sleep for the first time in over a week. Bob had fixed Neil's small portable radio to the roof of Mickey's pen where he couldn't reach it – just in case he tried to change the channel with his teeth.

The heating had been fixed at Meadowbank School so it was back to school on Tuesday –

unless any more pipes burst, which is what everyone was praying for. At break that day, Neil told his friends Chris and Hasheem all about Sherlock.

"He sounds terrific," Hasheem said. "I wish I could see him in action."

"Yes. I'd love to see what police dogs can do," Chris said longingly.

Neil stared at his friend. "I think you've just given me a really good idea . . ." he said.

After school, Neil ran his idea past Emily. She thought it was great. "So you'd get someone from the police to give a talk about what police dogs do," she confirmed.

Neil nodded energetically. "Yup."

"Then have a demonstration here at the kennels, and get Mr Harding to bring Sherlock . . ."

"Correct. That way Sergeant Moorhead can see how good he is," Neil said. "I'm sure Compton's very own dog handler will want to give a talk."

"Even if he hasn't got a dog at the moment?" said Emily pointedly.

Neil grimaced. "Depends on how soon we can do it. Obviously, I'd like to do it before Oliver arrives," he said.

"Who's going to come along to the demonstration? You can't invite the whole of Compton – we haven't got room!"

"I thought we could restrict it to two or three classes from school," Neil suggested. His own, Chris's and Emily's, for instance . . .

"Do you think Mum and Dad will agree?" asked Emily.

"I'm sure they will," Neil said. "They're as keen on Sergeant Moorhead having Sherlock as we are. They've really come round to the idea that Mr Harding is a reformed character."

Bob Parker was out, so Neil went to find his mother. He discovered her in the office, with Bev and Kate. All three looked downcast.

"What's wrong?" Neil asked in concern.

"It's this, Neil," Kate said, waving a letter in the air. "The RSPCA want me to go for an interview on Friday."

"Oh, no!" said Neil. He knew it was the wrong thing to say as soon as he saw Kate's stricken face. He could tell she felt torn in two over it. "Well, good luck, then," he said reluctantly, and backed out of the room.

He was wondering what to do next when he heard the sound of a dog coughing. When he went to investigate in Kennel Block Two, he found Pepé having another one of his turns. He ran back to the office to alert the others.

Mike Turner's phone number was engaged and his mobile was taking messages only.

"We'd better take Pepé right round there," Carole instructed.

Bob had taken the car, so Carole ran for the Range Rover. Neil jumped in beside her and Bev handed him a carrier containing Pepé.

Janice, Mike's veterinary nurse, greeted them at the surgery with a sympathetic glance towards Pepé. "Poor little mite," she murmured when she saw the quivering chihuahua. "He's so cute. Mike's doing an emergency operation at the moment, so I'll just find Pepé's notes. I can give him an injection, if that's what worked last time."

It worked extremely quickly and by the time Mike appeared from the operating theatre, Pepé was almost back to normal.

"Did you see anything this time?" he said to Carole.

She shook her head. "We were all in the office when it happened, I'm afraid. We can't watch him all the time and we did change his basket and check his food like you said."

"OK. When's his owner coming for him?"

asked Mike. "I really need to do these tests."

"On Sunday," Neil told him.

"Then I think you'll just have to set up a closed-circuit TV camera to try and film what's going on," said Mike. "Something is definitely bothering him."

Neil had just started to say, "Hey, Mum, that's not a bad idea," when he realized the vet was only joking.

It had been another close call and they were nowhere nearer to finding out the solution. It was another thing to add to Neil's list of things that were bothering him. He wanted to find a way to persuade Kate to stay at King Street Kennels *and* he still had to broach the subject of the police dog display with his parents.

Chapter Seven

Mr Hamley, Meadowbank School's head teacher, had a scatty Dalmatian bitch called Dotty. He loved dogs, but in small doses, and Dotty's recent litter had proved a bit much for Mr Hamley and his wife on top of their newborn son. So Neil was careful how he phrased his plan for the police dog demonstration when he suggested it to him on Wednesday.

As it happened, he had no need to worry. Mr Hamley thought the idea was great – very educational. He was sure he would go up a notch or two in the school governors' estimation, and Neil was only too willing to give him credit for his idea. After all, he had a different motive, and there might be a better chance of the demonstration happening if Mr Hamley was to ring the police and be the one to put the suggestion to them.

He and Emily had been right in guessing that their parents would raise no objections. Their father even offered to give the exercise field its first haircut of the year with the big sit-on mower.

"Shouldn't you have asked Mr Harding what he thought about showing Sherlock off before making all these plans?" Bob Parker asked Neil.

"Yes, of course I should. I didn't think," Neil said sheepishly.

"I can't see that he'll raise any objection," Bob continued. "Not if it might result in finding Sherlock a home with Sergeant Moorhead. As a matter of fact, I'm calling round to see him tonight. I'm thinking of starting an advanced obedience class and there are one or two questions on dog-training I need to ask him. Would you like to come?"

"Magic!" Neil told his father. It was a very good sign that Bob was actually going to see Mr Harding of his own accord. It showed that he was beginning to like him more – or at least admire his skill with dogs.

At Forthlyn Grove later that evening, Bob and Neil were greeted by two dogs trying to open the door between them. Jessie and Sherlock. A smartly dressed Barbara stood behind them. "Good job I'm a dog lover," she commented, "otherwise I'd get sick of removing dog hairs from my business suits."

"What do you do, exactly?" Bob enquired, while Neil was patting Sherlock and Jessie.

"Didn't James tell you? I own the bridal shop in Padsham. It's the only one for miles, so I don't do badly! I'm planning to put in some money to help set up James's new dog-breeding business, if we can find premises for it."

"Maybe I can help you find somewhere, if you tell me exactly what you need," Bob offered. "That's where our website comes in handy."

This is getting better and better, thought Neil. It would be great to see Mr Harding succeed at what he was best at: training dogs. He certainly hadn't succeeded at being an antiques thief! Neil fed Jessie a dog treat. She was one of his favourite dogs ever, but Sherlock was quickly endearing himself to Neil too, especially when he put a paw gently on his knee and lowered his head for Neil to scratch behind his ears. His amber eyes were the brightest that Neil had ever seen – full of warmth, intelligence and playfulness. He really was a very special dog.

When Neil brought up the idea of the police dog demonstration, Mr Harding was very enthusiastic. "Let me know the date as soon as you can, so I can have Sherlock looking his very best," he said. He asked Neil how Sam was and seemed genuinely relieved to find out that he hadn't suffered any ill effects from his sudden burst of activity.

"Mrs Harding said you wanted to start breeding dogs," Neil said. He was dying to hear more.

"Yes, that's right. I'd like to breed working

dogs such as German shepherds and spaniels, and train them."

"Spaniels?" queried Neil. "Why spaniels?"

"They're used by the Customs and Excise departments at airports and seaports as they're good at sniffing out consignments of drugs," Harding explained.

"I suppose the police won't have you back as a trainer now," Bob Parker said.

Harding shook his head. "Not now that I've got a criminal record. I still don't see why I can't work as a private trainer, though, and I can do that to a very high and professional standard."

Much to Neil's surprise, when they got up to go, Bob said, "Well, thanks for the tea, Barbara. Goodbye, James, be seeing you."

His father's use of their first names was a really good sign, Neil realized. Pity his mother was still so suspicious of Mr Harding, though. The only thing that could bring her round was dogs. If Harding were to start his business, she'd be bound to show some interest in that, surely . . .

On Thursday morning, Mr Hamley made a surprise announcement during assembly.

"I'm pleased to announce a special event for

all Meadowbank dog lovers," he said, standing on stage at the front of the hall.

Neil's eyes scanned the hall for Emily, Chris and Hasheem and they all exchanged excited glances.

"The police dog section have agreed to do some demonstrations specially for our school," continued Mr Hamley. "Inspector Williams, who is head of the dog section in this area, will give a talk on the work of police dogs, and you'll get the chance to see a police dog being put through his paces by his trainer. You all know Compton's very own police dog expert, Sergeant Moorhead? Well, he'll be there on the day too, to answer any questions you may have."

Mr Hamley tapped the lectern for quiet. "We've been able to arrange the first demonstration at very short notice. It will take place tomorrow afternoon at King Street Kennels," Mr Hamley continued. "We'll draw lots to decide who'll be going and you can take consent forms home this evening. Those unlucky enough not to attend this event will have the opportunity to see another similar demonstration later in the year."

Neil's brain did some swift calculations. Sergeant Moorhead had told them that he would be getting Oliver at the weekend. The demonstration was due to take place on Friday, so it looked as if his dream of getting Sherlock and Sergeant Moorhead together before Oliver came on the scene was about to come true!

That night, Neil and Emily helped their father tidy the exercise field and modernize Sam's old agility course. Sergeant Moorhead came down to inspect it and to offer them advice, and together they succeeded in constructing a very professional-looking course for the police dog demonstration.

After the sergeant had left, Neil and Emily accompanied their mother on a trip into Compton to the supermarket. As they pulled away from the car park, the Range Rover laden with groceries, Neil asked a question that had been niggling away at him. "Mum, if the police are meant to be running the event, will they let Sherlock go over the course, too?" he asked worriedly.

"Don't worry!" she said reassuringly. "Your dad has already phoned Inspector Williams about it. He doesn't mind at all if we put a couple of our own dogs round the course."

Neil grinned with relief. "Let's put Jake over

it, for a laugh," he said. "Every show needs a comedian!"

"I don't think so!" said Carole. Then she frowned. "It's a shame about Kate having her interview tomorrow afternoon. We really need every bit of help we can get."

"Couldn't she ask them to change the day?" Emily asked hopefully.

Neil felt the same way. It depressed him every time he thought about Kate and her interview. It seemed that she just didn't want to listen to any argument that might help persuade her to stay at King Street.

"I don't think she wants to change it, to be honest," said Carole. "This business has taken so much emotional energy out of all of us that I think she just wants it over with now. We all do. But she has promised to come straight back as soon as it's over."

Suddenly Emily stabbed a finger at the window. "Oh, look, Neil!"

The car was going past Compton police station and Neil turned round to see what his sister had noticed. Sergeant Moorhead was getting out of a van – with a dog. A young German shepherd. His heart sank. "Oh no," he groaned. "That must be Oliver!"

Carole slowed the vehicle a little and everyone craned across to look at the new arrival.

"This is a disaster!" said Emily. "Oliver wasn't expected until Sunday!"

"Sergeant Moorhead didn't mention anything earlier on about him getting Oliver tonight!" cried Neil. "Just look at him."

They all watched as the well-built German shepherd obeyed the sergeant's commands to follow him through into the station building.

Neil had to admit to himself that the dog looked healthy and well-muscled. He was very athletic-looking too for such a young dog. This was Neil's worst nightmare. All of their efforts might now be in vain.

As soon as he got home, Neil told his father what they had seen at the police station. "We might as well cancel the demonstration now," Neil said miserably.

"Of course we can't!" exclaimed Bob. "Your schoolmates would be really disappointed and we can't mess the police around just like that. They have no idea about your reasons for wanting this show so badly."

"But there's no point in having it now," said

Neil glumly. "It's too late! The whole thing was about getting Sergeant Moorhead together with Sherlock, but he's got Oliver now."

"It's never too late," Bob insisted. "The sergeant and Oliver may not get on. That's what being a dog handler's all about – the right dog with the right man. It's like a marriage. It needs the right chemistry, and Oliver and Sergeant Moorhead may not have it."

"I hope they haven't," Neil replied.

"They're bound to see Sherlock's talent, anyway," added Bob.

"I haven't got anything *against* Oliver," said Neil. "I haven't even met him yet and he does look a great dog. But I really, *really* want Sherlock to be Compton's police dog and I thought I'd cracked it when I had the idea for the demonstration. I feel really choked now."

Bob shrugged. "Life's not always very fair," he commented.

"No, it certainly isn't," Neil agreed. "If it was, Jasper wouldn't have been killed and Sergeant Moorhead wouldn't have to find his killer." He paused and heaved a great sigh. Then he got to his feet. "I'm off to take Sam for a walk," he said. He needed some fresh air and to work through his agitated feelings. Sam's calm presence was the perfect medicine for his troubles.

While the agility course was laid out for the demonstration the following day, Neil thought it best to take Sam everywhere on a lead. Otherwise no one could have kept him off it!

"It's only for a couple more days, boy," said Neil, stroking Sam's gleaming black back. Sam thumped his plumy tail on the ground and looked pointedly through the gate at the objects in the field.

"No, I *can't* let you in there," Neil said softly. "You and I will have to go for a walk in the woods instead."

Apart from two or three established tracks, the woods that ran along the length of the ridgeway were wild and steep and in some places quite impassable. When he was younger, Neil and his friend Chris Turner had spent many happy hours drawing adventure maps of the woods, filling in caves and inventing treasure, bears, wolves and even the occasional yeti.

Today, Neil and Sam took one of the regular paths. He walked slowly so that Sam wouldn't tire himself by climbing too fast. He had exercised Jake earlier to allow himself this quality time with Sam.

As he walked back towards home in the dying light, he found himself thinking about Sherlock. The dog was far too talented at police work to spend his life as a mere pet. Not that Mr Harding would let him go to somebody who would pamper and spoil him. He'd be more likely to keep him himself. But surely some police force somewhere would recognize his talent and be prepared to take him on?

Maybe Inspector Williams, the head of dog training, would talent-spot him. If he couldn't become the Compton police dog, maybe the Colshaw or Padsham forces would have him. But then Neil wouldn't see him any more. No, Sherlock *had* to become Compton's police dog.

Chapter Eight

I t seemed strange to Neil to have to spend Friday morning in school as usual, then come back to his own home accompanied by a teacher!

The weather forecast predicted a dry afternoon so Mr Hamley and Mrs Sharpe, his class teacher, helped unload the school PA system from the school bus to set up in the field. Bob had borrowed stacks of folding chairs from Gavin Thorpe at the church hall and set them up in neat lines.

Just after two o'clock, Inspector Williams, head of the area police dog section, began his talk, flanked by two experienced police dog handlers and their dogs. Both were German

shepherds – one was called Rusty and looked about six months older than Sherlock. She had just completed her basic training. The other was a much more mature dog aged three called Barney.

Neil stood to one side of the rows of chairs and watched his school friends as they eagerly absorbed the inspector's fascinating stories about life in the force with a dog. Mr Harding was in the audience at the back with Sherlock.

At intervals, while the inspector talked, Neil looked around anxiously towards the kennels. The most important person of the afternoon was still missing. Soon, Sherlock would get his chance to show what he was capable of, but without Sergeant Moorhead there to witness it, all the German shepherd's efforts – and Neil's, too – would be wasted.

Inspector Williams finished his talk and was greeted with a spontaneous round of applause.

Then Neil's father announced that, first of all, a local dog would be put round the course and asked to display some tracking skills. This would be followed by a demonstration by the trained police dogs. There was an outbreak of excited chattering. This was what everyone had been looking forward to – a chance to see dogs in action.

Neil went and stood next to Mr Harding and Sherlock, who looked eager and raring to go. "It must be difficult for a dog to follow a scent in wet grass," he remarked to Mr Harding. "Isn't it easier if the grass is dry?"

To his surprise, Mr Harding told him wet grass held a scent longer than dry grass. "A dog has to be able to find a person or an object as long as two hours after the scent has been laid. They have to rest their noses every twenty minutes if they're tracking over a long distance. Their sense of smell is about two hundred times better than that of a human being."

At last, everybody was settled and it was time for Sherlock to start the demonstration. Neil saw interest in the eyes of the police dog handlers as the handsome young German shepherd came up to the course. Mr Harding gave him a pat, then set him at the first obstacle. Sherlock was like an Olympic athlete. He seemed to take wings as he did his long jump. He cleared the three metres easily. He flew over the hurdle and managed the plank sure-footedly.

When he came to the wall, the dog prepared for his leap like a horse would do in the show-jumping ring. He sized it up, then took a run up to it, followed by a mighty jump that took him in one bound almost to the very top. One heave and he was on the ridge, then down the other side, to a round of applause.

Then Mr Harding had an opportunity to show how well Sherlock could track. Mr Harding asked for a volunteer and Hasheem Lindon was the first to put up his hand and dash onto the field. Neil's friend let Sherlock have a good sniff of him, then was instructed to lose himself in the crowd while Sherlock's vision was covered. Hasheem sat right at the back of the spectators, but as soon as Mr

Harding issued a command, Sherlock went virtually straight to him.

Brilliant! thought Neil. *That dog's just incredible! If only Sergeant Moorhead could have seen him,* Neil thought agonizingly. Then he reminded himself that there were other representatives of the dog section here, including the area head man himself. Surely they would know a first class police dog when they saw one?

Sherlock's performance earned him a round of cheers and noisy applause. People clamoured to make a fuss of him and the inspector came up to talk to Mr Harding.

Suddenly, Neil noticed someone else in uniform taking a close interest in Sherlock. Someone with another German shepherd in a harness and on a lead. *Sergeant Moorhead!* thought Neil triumphantly.

How long had he been there? Neil could only assume that he had arrived while he had been concentrating on watching Sherlock's accomplished performance on the field. He hoped that the sergeant had witnessed the whole of Sherlock's performance.

Inspector Williams made a further announcement. "I think we were *all* impressed with Sherlock. A splendid example of dedicated training – and very much like the real thing!"

Hear, hear, thought Neil.

It was now time for the high spot of the demonstration, when one of the fully-trained police dogs, Barney, gave his display. This included the "chase and attack" technique, in which a dog caught a human quarry. The police officer who was to play the role of criminal had padding round his arm just in case, though the dogs were trained not to bite too hard.

The police officer raced down the field, then Barney was released and hurtled after him. Everyone gasped as the man pretended to fight Barney and the German shepherd held on to his arm until his own handler could reach the spot. It was a thrilling moment.

After both dogs had excelled over the agility course with flawless performances, the police team answered lots of questions. Finally, Mr Hamley gave a speech thanking the police and Bob Parker.

Neil listened impatiently. He was dying to tear himself away from his parents and go over to where Mr Harding was now talking to Sergeant Moorhead! As soon as Mr Hamley had finished, Neil excused himself and dashed off.

He found the sergeant looking Sherlock over. "He's a fine animal. Very fine," he said, rubbing Sherlock's furry chest. The German shepherd put up a paw and rested it on the sergeant's arm. *It's almost as if he's saying "take me home with you"*, thought Neil.

"I was most impressed with the way he tracked," continued the sergeant, as he scratched behind Sherlock's ears. Sherlock put his head on one side, his broad pink tongue lolling. He looked as if he were lapping up the praise.

"Yes. Isn't he brilliant?" said Neil brightly. "Don't you think he'd make a first-rate police dog?"

"I think he would," added Emily, who had just joined them.

"Definitely," Sergeant Moorhead said. Mr Harding shot Neil a triumphant look and Neil gave him a thumbs-up sign behind the police sergeant's back. "I know Inspector Williams has already had a word with you about him. He'd like you to bring him to the training centre for a proper assessment – that is, if you're willing to part with him and allow the police to have him," he added.

"That's what I want most for him," Mr Harding confirmed.

Inspector Williams and his colleagues stayed for a while to chat to the pupils of Meadowbank School and let them meet the dogs. Lots of people wanted to pet Sherlock and Oliver.

Neil went to fetch Jake to let him stretch his legs. A few pats and strokes would be just what he was looking for!

As he opened the gate to the courtyard, he spotted Mr Harding talking to his father.

Suddenly, a shrill scream set all the dogs yapping. "A rat! I saw a rat in there," Mrs Sharpe shouted, pointing towards the feed store, the door of which was slightly open. Neil guessed that Bev must have been getting things ready for the evening feeds.

Suddenly, Mr Harding pointed towards the door. "Search," he ordered Sherlock.

As several people gathered round to watch the unfolding excitement, the young German shepherd nosed the door fully open and slipped inside. Then a sound came from inside the storeroom, a kind of high-pitched yelp.

"He's caught it," Mrs Sharpe said excitedly.

Seconds later, Sherlock emerged with something brown and fluffy held gently by the scruff of its neck in his mouth. He dropped it at Mr Harding's feet. It was very big for a rat. The small furry creature stood up, shook itself and gave a yap which was distinctly canine. It was Pepé.

"Bad dog!" said Carole. The tiny chihuahua looked sheepish as she scooped him up. "I don't understand how he got out," said Carole worriedly. "It's never happened before."

"We'd better examine his pen before we put him back," Neil said.

At first glance, everything seemed fine. But when Neil actually felt the wire netting all over, he discovered that it was loose in the bottom right-hand corner, perhaps forced by a par-

ticularly strong dog that had inhabited the pen before him. No normal-sized dog could have squeezed through the tiny hole, but Pepé wasn't a normal-sized dog.

"So that's how he escaped," exclaimed Emily. "What a devil!"

Pepé and his things were quickly transferred to a spare pen until the netting could be fixed at a later date. Then Neil, Carole and Bev went to inspect the damage in the feed store.

Kate had just returned from her interview and looked startled by all the attention Pepé was receiving. "What's going on?" she wanted to know.

When Neil told her, he saw Kate looking thoughtfully at the sack of hamster food on the floor. It had neat little holes in the bottom and was leaking seeds and nuts. "I wonder . . ." she said. "I think I'll consult Mike about this, Neil."

"About what?" Neil enquired, mystified.

"Just an idea of mine. I'll tell you when I find out if I'm right or wrong," she promised. Then she walked out and got on with her job again before Neil had a chance to ask her how her interview had gone. He set off after her, then spotted Mr Harding and Sergeant Moorhead coming across the courtyard towards him.

"Is your father anywhere around?" the sergeant asked Neil.

"I think I saw him going over to the barn," Neil replied. Sherlock stuck his nose in Neil's hand. "Good boy," Neil said, giving him a pat. Sherlock thumped Neil's leg with his thick tail.

The sergeant's radio squawked and he started talking into it. Neil listened intently, knowing that he really shouldn't. "Yes . . . yes . . . Folly Lane . . . Empty, you say? Right, I'm on my way."

He turned to Neil and Mr Harding. "The car's turned up," he told them. His face was set in a fierce scowl. "Maybe this time I'll get the man who killed Jasper. Come on, Oliver."

As the sergeant rushed towards his car, Mr Harding shouted, "Two dogs are better than one. I'll follow you," and made for his car.

Neil looked around for either of his parents but they were not within earshot. "Let me come, too," Neil begged. Like the sergeant and Mr Harding, he was just as anxious to see Jasper's killer brought to justice. Also, he longed to see Sherlock and Oliver involved in some real police action.

But Mr Harding dashed his hopes. "No," he said curtly. "I'm not taking you, and that's that.

I'm in enough trouble with your parents already for all the danger I put you in after the antiques robberies. I want them to be able to trust me now so we can all get on in the future. The dog business world is a small one and I want to get a good reputation. I won't do that if I do something irresponsible and reckless, like taking you off on a hunt for a criminal!"

Neil stood his ground. "I'll take responsibility for myself, don't worry about that. I'll say I forced you to take me along with you. Dad knows how persuasive I can be."

"Look, I've got to go now or I'll never catch them up. For the last time, Neil, you're not coming."

"Oh yes, I am!" said Neil determinedly, opening the passenger door. He saw his sister and yelled, "Em, I'm going back with Mr Harding for a while . . ."

He would face the consequences later. For now, all Neil wanted was to be with Sherlock when Jasper's murderer was caught.

Chapter Nine

In the eerie half-light, as afternoon began to fade into evening, Neil and Mr Harding drove along the twisting country road and climbed out of Compton towards the woods. Neil clutched the dashboard nervously as they rounded each bend, desperately trying to keep Sergeant Moorhead's police car in his sight. Behind him, Sherlock's eager panting tickled Neil's neck.

Then, turning a sweeping corner, they saw a longer stretch of road and found themselves the only car in the vicinity.

"We're here," said Mr Harding.

"Where have they gone?" Neil asked

anxiously. "We don't want to miss any of the action."

Folly Lane was a long, narrow road which skirted Compton Woods and had high banks on either side, topped by thick hedgerows.

Mr Harding slowed the car and crawled along the lane, just in case any police cars should speed towards them. The lane was dark as the trees met overhead in many places, forming a tunnel. They crested a hill and then saw two parked police cars next to what Neil assumed was the abandoned stolen car.

Mr Harding drew up behind them, stopped the car and opened the back door for Sherlock to jump out.

Sherlock nudged Neil with his nose and Neil gave him a reassuring pat. Another big test for him might be just round the corner and Neil didn't want the dog to be nervous.

"Neil," said Mr Harding, "I should really ask you to stay in the car. I don't know what's going to happen next."

Neil nodded but began walking towards a shadowy path that led into the trees. "I'm OK. I won't do anything stupid."

Mr Harding shrugged and set off after him, with Sherlock padding along between them.

Within a couple of minutes they came upon Sergeant Moorhead, Oliver and two other Compton police constables.

Neil nudged Mr Harding. "Look at that," he said. "The sergeant is giving Oliver something to sniff."

Up ahead, in a small clearing, Sergeant Moorhead was holding something out to the dog. It looked like a jacket.

At the sound of Neil's voice, he swivelled round.

"What *are* you doing, bringing Neil with you?" the sergeant said angrily. "This could be dangerous!"

Neil tensed. "I wouldn't let him leave without me," he admitted. "There wasn't much he could do about it. So here I am."

"No, Neil, I can't expose you to any danger, you know that. Stay behind with Constable Grey, here," Sergeant Moorhead insisted, nodding towards one of his men.

Neil frowned. He didn't *want* to stay behind and miss seeing the dogs at work. Then he looked at the garment the policeman was holding out to Oliver. "Did you find that jacket in the car?" Neil asked.

"Yes. We think it belongs to the man we're

after," said the sergeant.

"You believe he was working on his own, then?" Mr Harding asked.

"Yes. That's what our information is," Sergeant Moorhead replied.

Oliver was still sniffing at the jacket.

"Why don't you let Sherlock sniff it, too? You know how good he is at tracking," Neil said.

The sergeant looked up. "You're right. Two noses are better than one." Then he paused. "Though it is highly irregular. However, I know the inspector's keen to try Sherlock out."

Mr Harding took the jacket and held it out for Sherlock. The German shepherd's tail started to wag. He whimpered and strained on his lead, sniffing keenly. Sherlock was obviously eager to set off after the scent. Oliver was agitated too but was sitting quietly, awaiting orders. Neil thought about the two dogs' different personalities. Sherlock seemed far more extro-vert than Oliver, who was quieter and more reserved.

Sergeant Moorhead, the other constable – called Edwards – and Mr Harding set off with the two dogs. Neil peered impatiently after them. It was growing darker every minute. He strained his eyes and saw that the group had halted in the centre of the field. Suddenly, Neil heard the howl of a dog in trouble.

"Something's up!" cried Neil.

Constable Grey's eyes searched for the departed group amongst the trees. He shifted uncomfortably from one foot to the other.

Neil couldn't see what was wrong, but he *had* to find out. "Come on," he yelled and started to run into the trees.

Constable Grey shouted, "Oi! Come back," but instinctively raced after him.

When they drew level with the others, they found there was a stream flowing across the middle of the field. Recent rainstorms had swollen the waters so that now it was more like a river. In places, the water had spread out and formed shallow ponds all along its banks.

"Does anyone know if there's any way round this lot?" Sergeant Moorhead enquired.

"We could go further into the wood but it could be even more difficult to cross it there," said Neil quickly. He knew the woods very well because he walked Jake and Sam there so often at weekends. "The ground's steeper and rockier. We'd be scrambling over mossy stones and waterfalls. Both ways, we'd get equally wet."

Sergeant Moorhead seemed surprised to see Neil so soon. "Not you again. I thought I told you to stay put?" He shook his head. "I haven't got time for this!" He quickly turned his attention back to the immediate problem.

"We might as well cross here," said Mr Harding. "We should still be able to pick up the scent again on the other side." He and Sherlock waded carefully across. The water came up to the top of Sherlock's legs.

Neil splashed across after them, his trainers managing to get enough grip on the stream bed. He was scrambling up the bank on the other side when he heard a shout from behind and twisted round.

Sergeant Moorhead was standing in the middle of the stream, tugging forcibly on Oliver's lead. "Come on, Oliver!"

The German shepherd was pulling back, refusing to enter the water. He gave another forlorn howl like the one Neil had heard earlier.

"Let him off the lead," Neil suggested. "Maybe he wants to find his own way across."

Mr Harding nodded.

The sergeant sploshed back to Oliver and unclipped the lead. The German shepherd, whimpering miserably, backed even further away from the water, sat down and looked at the sergeant as if asking for help.

"Oliver, come on, it's all right," coaxed the sergeant. "What on earth's the matter with him?"

"Looks like he's scared of the water," Mr Harding said. "I think you'll have to carry him."

The sergeant and Constable Edwards lifted the struggling, heavy German shepherd between them and carried him to the far side. Once he was put safely down on the muddy bank he was a changed dog and seemed to recover his calm manner. But, during his troubles, he'd lost the scent and couldn't seem to pick it up again. By contrast, Sherlock was

straining on his lead, his nose desperately sniffing the ground.

They set off again, this time following Sherlock alone. "Water's not a set part of a police dog's training routine," Mr Harding informed everybody as they jogged along. "Sometimes you don't discover that a dog is afraid of water until a late stage. All dogs are natural swimmers, but, like people, some just don't like water."

"Can anything be done?" asked the sergeant breathlessly.

"Yes," Harding replied. "It can be sorted out. I'm sure I could help him overcome his fear."

"We'll talk about it later," the sergeant said. "Let's get on with the search, while Sherlock still has the scent. He's the only one who can help us now."

Neil tagged safely along at the back, alongside Constable Grey. The sergeant had insisted he try not to get under their feet as they tracked the potentially dangerous criminal.

Within minutes, they came to the end of another field and had to scramble through wire fencing before they were once more in the woods. Sherlock had been in the woods before and was let loose. He ran ahead and plunged into the trees. As Oliver was still unfamiliar with the terrain, he remained on Sergeant Moorhead's lead and under more control.

It was much darker now and all three policemen produced torches and shone them on the path ahead. Even with the extra light, it was still difficult to avoid tree roots and loose stones as they climbed through the hilly woods. Mr Harding told them how to get to a ruined house where he thought the man on the run might be heading. Harding had often walked Sherlock near here and had glimpsed it through the undergrowth.

Panting from the steepness and difficulty of the climb, they continued to make their way through the trees.

Suddenly, somewhere in the darkness way ahead of them, they heard an almost unearthly howling and barking which made the hairs along Neil's arms bristle.

"Sherlock's found something – or somebody," Harding said excitedly.

"Do you think Jasper's killer is still there?" asked Neil bitterly.

"He's either there, or he's been there recently," said Sergeant Moorhead. He looked down at his dog. "Oliver's picked up the scent again. Look!" The lean, muscular German shepherd had his nose to the ground and occasionally stopped to sniff a branch which the man might have grasped as he hauled his way up the hill.

Sherlock howled again, much closer this time.

Constable Edwards raised his hand. "Listen," he said.

They all stopped moving. Then Neil heard, quite distinctly, a man's voice swearing at Sherlock. Sherlock yelped and they heard something thudding in undergrowth quite close by. It sounded as if somebody was throwing rocks at the dog. Neil blazed with anger.

"Neil, stay here with Constable Grey," the sergeant barked. The constable looked at Neil somewhat resentfully. "Harding, Edwards, follow me."

Neil pretended he hadn't heard and shot forward with the others. Pushing their way through thick, prickly bushes, they found themselves at a ruined single-storey cottage. The thief had certainly chosen a good hiding place. Neil didn't think many people would be bothered to push their way through all those thorns just to explore.

A tree grew over the tumbledown walls, forming a makeshift roof. Sherlock was barking at a hole in a wall which had once formed a window. Constable Edwards stepped in front of Neil and swung his torch towards the black cavity.

There, illuminated in the blinding beam, was the face of a man of about thirty. He was unshaven and he had a black woollen hat pulled right down as far as his eyebrows.

"Call that dog off," he shouted desperately.

Neil could see the expression on Sergeant Moorhead's face. He had never, *ever* seen a man look so angry. At that moment, Neil realized how much the policeman had wanted to catch the man who had killed Jasper.

But he still had to be apprehended.

The police acted swiftly as a professional unit.

Mr Harding grabbed Sherlock's collar and Neil quickly took cover behind the huge, solid trunk of a beech tree nearby.

"Give it up!" Sergeant Moorhead ordered towards the cottage. "You can't get away now."

The man shouted defiantly but refused to emerge.

"Then we're coming in!" yelled the sergeant, his torch beam trained on the crumbling window. All three officers moved forwards, homing in on different entrances to the building.

Neil saw the man's face disappear inside. Then there was a clatter of loose stones and the man appeared again, on what was left of the roof. From there, he leapt up an overhanging branch and began to swing along it, hand over hand.

"Grab him!" Sergeant Moorhead yelled down to Oliver.

Neil drew a sharp intake of breath when he saw Sherlock, not Oliver, respond first with an enormous bound towards the ruined building. Jumping up, Sherlock gripped the man's left ankle in his fierce jaws.

The man yelled in pain and kicked out at the dog wildly, but the German shepherd's weight dragged the cursing man from his branch. He landed with a thump on the stony ground and rolled over. Immediately, he was jumped on by the two constables. Constable Edwards held the man's arms behind his back while Constable Grey clipped some handcuffs on to finally restrain him. Only then was Sherlock given the order by Mr Harding nearby to release his grip on the man's ankle.

"Well done, Sherlock, good dog," said Sergeant Moorhead, ruffling his fur vigorously. Sherlock tilted his head, then butted the sergeant's hand with his nose and licked it. *They like each other*, thought Neil. Oliver, too, was given a pat so that he wouldn't feel left out, but there was no doubt in anyone's mind that all the glory belonged to Sherlock.

The constables frisked the prostrate burglar. Zipped into the inside pocket of his jacket they found a plastic bag containing the stolen watches and jewellery.

"Thanks for lending us Sherlock," the sergeant told Mr Harding. "He really has been an asset on this job. I've known dogs who've graduated from dog training college who wouldn't have had the intelligence to size up the situation and bring that man down from the tree. All credit to you, Harding. And to Sherlock, of course." He bent down and ruffled the dog's neck fur.

Neil watched as the sergeant stroked and patted Sherlock again. He seemed very pleased. Neil felt sure they would easily bond – if only they got the chance. He was so proud of Sherlock and couldn't help smiling when he saw the beaming face of an equally proud Mr Harding.

Sergeant Moorhead stood up and moved in front of the burglar, whose arms were gripped by a sturdy constable on either side. "As for you," he said to the quaking man, who hung his head, "you deserve to go to prison for what you did to my dog! And I hope you do."

Chapter Ten

"**A**nd just where have you been?" Bob Parker thundered as Neil nervously opened the passenger door of Mr Harding's car, back at King Street. "You told Emily you were going home with Mr Harding and you'd be back *soon*. That was more than two hours ago!"

Neil's dad turned to Harding, who was letting Sherlock out of the car. "We rang several times and your wife said you weren't back yet. We've been really worried. What's been going on?"

"Allow me to explain—" began Mr Harding, but Neil broke in.

"Sorry, Dad," he said. "Sergeant Moorhead got a message to say they'd found the car that was driven by the man who killed Jasper. He took Oliver to see if there was any scent for him to follow and Mr Harding decided to follow him in case Sherlock could help out."

"How dare you take my son with you!" Bob boomed, facing Mr Harding. "It could have been really dangerous!"

"Please, Dad. It wasn't Mr Harding's fault, it was mine. I insisted he took me with him. I got in the car and wouldn't get out. He didn't have any choice," Neil admitted.

"You *lied* to Emily, too," Bob continued angrily. "I'm sure you could have stopped him getting into your car, James," he accused Harding.

Mr Harding shrugged and sighed. "Sorry, Bob, but once your son gets an idea into his head, there's nothing you can do with him," he said.

"*Tell me about it*," Neil's father replied grimly. "But I don't expect a responsible adult to encourage him and—"

"He didn't encourage me. Oh Dad, it was great! Sherlock caught the burglar and I was never in any danger because the police made me stay behind a tree. Poor old Oliver, though. He really let himself down. He wouldn't cross the stream. It turns out he's afraid of water. So what we did was—"

Bob Parker threw up his hands. "I give up!" He sighed heavily. "Please promise me you'll never do anything foolhardy like that again," he snapped.

"Yes, Dad. Of course, Dad. When we got to the wood, we heard Sherlock howling like a wolf. It was amazing! So we . . ." As Neil continued eagerly describing the happenings of the last two hours, they gradually moved towards the house, where Carole, Emily and Sarah were standing in the doorway, waiting to hear what had happened.

At the end of Neil's story, Sherlock was heavily patted and praised and even given a dog treat by Carole – a rare honour indeed! "He really is a wonder dog," she said. "The way he pulled that burglar out of the tree! I'm really, really glad that they've got the man who killed Jasper at last. Poor Sergeant Moorhead . . ."

They all went quiet for a moment, thinking of Jasper. Then Carole said, "Tell me, James, what do you plan to do to get Oliver over his phobia?"

"Well, if the police allow me, I plan to introduce him to water gradually. Something like a small paddling pool at first," Harding explained. "I'd let him see Jessie playing in it so he can see that water can be fun. It's my theory that perhaps something happened to him when he was a puppy. Maybe he was forced to have a bath, or fell in a pond, and it was an unpleasant, scary experience for him. Who knows? He's a good dog. I'm sure it would be worth it."

"If you can't do it, who can?" said Neil. "Look how well you've trained Sherlock and Jessie!"

Both Carole and Bob nodded their approval.

Mum's getting to like him at last! Neil thought cheerfully.

Neil got up late the next morning, after a night full of dreams involving Sherlock chasing burglars through woods. By the time he had eaten his breakfast and walked Sam and Jake, Mike Turner had arrived to start his regular Saturday morning clinic. Just as Neil was crossing the courtyard to have a word with Mike, Kate called him over. She was looking happier than she had done for a long time.

"Neil, Neil . . . listen to this!" she said, waving a sheet of paper.

Oh, no, he thought, *she's been offered the*

RSPCA job! "Did you get it, then?" he asked her.

Kate frowned. "Get what? Oh, you mean the job. I'll tell you about that in a minute. No, these are Pepé's allergy test results. I had a hunch that he might be allergic to nuts because there were some in the hamster food. Lots of people have nut allergies, so I thought, why not dogs? I mentioned it to Mike and he took samples from Pepé yesterday and got his allergy specialist friend to rush the analysis through."

"I thought Mike said he had to wait till Pepé's owner got back?" Neil asked.

"True, but he realized that if I was right, Pepé's owner should be told right away," Kate explained. "Imagine if she had a welcome home party and Pepé got his nose in a bowl of peanuts and started scoffing them, and had another turn? These things are best identified as soon as possible. Anyway, I was right! There's a certain type of mould that can grow on raw peanuts, and *that's* what he's allergic to."

"Will he be OK?"

"He'll be fine – just so long as he keeps away from them. Mike's got a leaflet on allergies for us to give Pepé's owner."

Bev had joined them while they were talking. "You're a genius, Kate," she said. "I'd never have thought of the peanut connection." Kate smiled a glowing smile and Bev carried on towards the kennel blocks.

"Now, tell me how the interview went," Neil said nervously once they were alone again. He didn't know how much Kate had already told the others.

Kate blushed. "OK, I think."

Worse luck, thought Neil. "So that means, if they offer you the job, you'll go?" he asked. But the answer was quite the opposite to the one he was expecting.

"No," said Kate.

"What do you mean, no?" Neil asked. He couldn't believe what he was hearing.

"Exactly that. Whether they offer it to me or not, I'm not leaving King Street Kennels." Kate folded her arms and looked at him, her lips twitching slightly.

Neil stared at her. "Why not?" he asked her.

"It's all your fault," she told him. "Remember that day you and Emily were trying to persuade me to stay?"

"Yes," Neil said. How could he forget? He'd seldom felt such a failure.

"That's when I realized I didn't want another kennel maid doing my job. I love working here, with you and the dogs. I can't imagine being this happy anywhere else."

Wow, thought Neil happily. All this time, he'd been positive that Kate had turned deaf ears to what he and Em had said that day. But she hadn't. She'd actually listened and thought about it. *What a result!*

"It was stupid of me to feel I wasn't needed," Kate continued. "Just because you'd taken on Bev as well. There's more than enough work for the two of us. And I *like* Bev. We're really good friends now. So I hope you don't mind putting up with me for a while longer . . ." Kate's eyes danced.

Neil let his happy grin say how he felt.

There was a queue of people with their dogs waiting to see Mike. Neil popped his head in and asked for the leaflet about allergies as he wanted to research the facts. He was becoming so interested in dogs' health that, not for the first time, he wondered if he might end up training to be a vet himself.

He sat on the wall by the barn and was reading up on allergy symptoms when he saw a police car coming down the drive. Sergeant Moorhead was at the wheel. Neil ran to greet him. The sergeant let Oliver out of the back and he ran up to Neil, wagging his tail.

"Hello, Oliver," Neil said, stroking the German shepherd's head. "Hi, Sergeant Moorhead."

"Oh, I see. Dogs first, humans second," the sergeant joked.

Neil gave an embarrassed grin.

"Don't worry, I quite agree with you," Sergeant Moorhead laughed. "Now, is Mr Harding here, by any chance? When I rang him earlier, he said he was dropping into King Street Kennels round about midday."

"I haven't seen him," Neil replied with a frown. He wondered why his parents hadn't told him. Unless, of course, Mr Harding's visit was an unofficial one and they didn't know.

The sound of a car alerted them both. It was Mr Harding and his wife, Barbara. He beeped his horn and Jessie and Sherlock barked a greeting from the back seat.

Neil was soon bending down to greet both dogs with an affectionate hug.

They all walked over to the kitchen, where Neil knew his father was reading his newspaper. "Oh, hello," he said, getting up from the table. "I wasn't expecting visitors . . ."

The large kitchen was suddenly full of dogs, as two German shepherds mingled with two

Border collies and one Airedale cross. Neil smiled happily as he was jostled by warm, hairy bodies and thumped by wagging tails. Hearing the commotion, Carole, Emily and Sarah all crowded into the kitchen too to find out what was happening. It felt as if there was a party going on.

"I came to thank you all for your help," announced Sergeant Moorhead. "And to tell you that the man we caught has been formally charged with committing the burglary. But that's not all," Sergeant Moorhead said. "The RSPCA are going to carry out their own private prosecution because of his deliberate cruelty to Jasper."

"That's really good news," exclaimed Bob.

Jessie had found her way to Carole's side. Carole stroked her and held on to her collar so that there would be one less wandering dog to trip everybody up. Jake had found Jessie, whom he adored, and was snuggled up next to her, lying across Barbara Harding's foot.

"I spoke to Inspector Williams this morning," the sergeant told Mr Harding. "He wants to know if you could bring Sherlock over to the training school in Padsham on Tuesday, so that he can try him out."

"Sure," responded Harding.

"What about Oliver?" asked Neil.

"Well, I've recommended to the inspector that, as Mr Harding has special skills with dogs, he should be officially appointed to help finish off his training and see if he can cure him of his water aversion. What do you say, Mr Harding?"

"If he makes the offer, I'll be only too happy to accept," said Mr Harding. "My first official customer! I think Oliver and I could work well together. What do you say, boy?"

Mr Harding fondled the ears of the tall, strong German shepherd and Oliver leant against Mr Harding's legs and licked his hand. Neil could see that the dog trusted and accepted Mr Harding. That was the first hurdle overcome.

Neil spoke the burning question that was on everybody's minds. "But nobody knows how long Oliver's special training will take, Sergeant. And you need another dog fairly soon. What are the chances of you being allowed to have Sherlock?"

The policeman smiled. "Extremely good, I should think," he replied. "He'll need to complete another three-week police dog training course where I'm sure he'll do well – especially after the excellent start Mr Harding's given him. But there's another important factor to take into consideration, too . . ." He paused and looked round at everyone.

Emily couldn't wait for him to continue. "What's that?" she prompted eagerly.

The sergeant laughed. "I think we've taken to one another!" he said, scratching Sherlock's head. The German shepherd's amber eyes glowed as he looked up at the sergeant. Neil knew love between dog and man when he saw it. He felt sure that the two were well on their way to becoming as inseparable as the sergeant and Jasper had once been.

"Brilliant!" yelled Neil.

Everybody laughed.

"Well done, Sherlock," Neil said, giving the dog a big pat. "Jasper would be really proud of you."

Sherlock barked his agreement.